Joy and Pain
(Latter Rain Series: Book 3)

I0659142

Adrienne Thompson

Pink Cashmere Publishing

Arkansas, USA

Cover art by AA Thompson (thompson9699@gmail.com)

Printed in the United States of America

First Printing 2016

Copyright © 2016 Adrienne Thompson

ISBN: 0-9971461-5-X
ISBN-13: 978-0-9971461-5-8

"If I have the gift of prophecy and can fathom all mysteries and all knowledge, and if I have a faith that can move mountains, but do not have love, I am nothing."
1 Corinthians 13:2 NIV

Soundtrack provided by Maze featuring Frankie Beverly:

"Changing Times"

"While I'm Alone"

"Ain't it Strange"

"Welcome Home"

"Workin' Together"

"Reason"

"Timin'"

"Feel That You're Feelin'"

"Love Is The Key"

"Family"

"Reachin' Down Inside"

"The Morning After"

"Love Is"

"We Are One"

"Happy Feelin's"

"Joy and Pain"

"I Love You Too Much"

You can listen to the *Joy and Pain* soundtrack on YouTube.

Prologue

Rosa

One thing life has taught me is that things happen in their own time, and often that time is not the time you expected. I met Lawrence Noble when I least expected it. I was a school teacher back then. Not because it had been some dream of mine to teach, but because I was a young black woman who grew up in the country and that was the only option I saw for myself in the early seventies. Nevertheless, I grew to enjoy my job and love my kindergarten students. Lawrence was the father of one of my students.

He was also married.

I was fresh out of school—just twenty-two when we met. Lawrence was thirty and handsome. He owned a local gas station and a couple more in neighboring towns. I'm not going to sit here and lie and say I fell in love with him, because I didn't.

I fell in *lust*.

And three months after our little affair began, I found out I was pregnant with our child, a little boy I'd name Freeman Stark—Man, for short. Those were the old days and my little hometown was the buckle of the Bible belt, so I was scorned by the community, lost my job, and eventually left Hyacinth Valley. I didn't return for several years. The older folks that had looked down on me were mostly gone by the time I did return. So was Lawrence and his family.

Man was grown and I was a mature woman with second sight and enough life experiences to fill three or four books, but I had never been in love.

And to be honest, I had no desire to ever be in love. No desire at all.

1
"Changing Times"

August was gone. He and his wife, Von, were in Paris, I think. They were hard to keep up with. Rochelle and her family were in LA. Ms. Dorcas's wedding was in less than a month and then she'd be gone, too. That left the young man I'd hired to replace August, who was not even half the worker or man he was, Dee Dee, and me. For the first time since I returned home and bought the place, I was seriously considering closing it down. But then I thought about all of the love that had been found there and the lives that had been changed there and pushed those thoughts of giving up out of my head. But I needed to hire some more help and the problem with that was that God had given me the gift of discernment among other things. I could read people a mile away; meaning, I instantly knew if they weren't trustworthy and so far I hadn't found even one honest person. I knew I could train Dee Dee to do Rochelle's job, but did I really want to spend that much time with her? That girl could grate on your nerves sometimes talking about all of her "cousins."

Anyway, I had a lot on my mind, too much to be concerned about the fact that I'd recently spent the night in Room Ten. Besides, I always knew when someone's love was coming, saw them before *they* even knew they'd come here. I didn't see any love coming for me.

I pored over the applications and resumes until my head began to hurt, and then I called it a day and headed to my room since we had no guests.

**

That night, I dreamt about the legend behind Room Ten—the story that few people knew. I dreamt about a slave girl named Essie who fell in love with the master's son. Essie was a house slave with beautiful ebony skin, acquired from a neighboring plantation to settle a debt. She was smart, a hard worker, and quickly caught the eye of her master's son, who was promised to a girl who lived in Mississippi. His name was Richard Jarsdel, and he was handsome and very well-mannered and actually treated the lovely Essie like a human being, desired her for the woman she was, and very swiftly fell in love with her.

And she fell in love with his kind heart and handsome face. He was her master's son, which made him her master as well, and if he was like other masters and masters' sons, he would've just taken her body, used her until he grew tired of her, and then forgotten her. But Richard Jarsdel was not like other masters or other masters' sons. He loved her genuinely and desired her fully, not just for her body. It didn't take long for the desire to overtake them both and right there in Room Ten, which at the time was Richard's room, they secretly took vows to be forever devoted to one another and consummated their love.

The next morning, Richard's mother, Hannah, caught them in bed together and pitched a fit, shunned Essie from the house and ordered that she be whipped for seducing her son and having the audacity to sleep in his bed, but Richard wouldn't have any of that. That very afternoon, he hitched up a wagon and left with his lady love. As the story is told, they eventually ended up settling in New York State where they raised a family together. Neither ever returned to Hyacinth Manor to live again. The legend holds that their love was so real and pure that it still lived on in that room even though both of them had long ago transitioned to Heaven. I had witnessed the power of that room time and time again and believed it was a place where not only love dwelled, but the spirit of God Himself. For only He could put together the love I'd seen develop between the most unlikely of people due to their connection to that room.

When I woke up in the small bedroom I claimed as my own, I felt a hollowing in my soul that I'd never felt before, as if something in me had been emptied out, but I had no idea what it was or how to get it back.

2
"While I'm Alone"

I decided I needed a break. I'd been scrambling around, trying to make arrangements for Dorcas's wedding and trying to hire new staff, things I'd depended on Rochelle to do over the years, and it had taken its toll on me. I was no youngster. I was sixty-two years old and when I overextended myself, I felt every single year. So I closed down the manor for a few days, gave my employees some time off, and just slept in the first day. Raided the refrigerator off and on and finished a good book I'd started weeks earlier. On the second day, I walked the grounds of the manor, ended up at August's old place out back, thought about how much I missed that boy and at the same time, how ecstatic I was that he'd found love and happiness.

On the third day, I left, drove the forty minutes it took to get to Ebbington, a little town that boasted a population of three thousand residents rather than the one thousand that lived in Hyacinth Valley. Ebbington was a tourist's town with lots of quaint little shops, including a fabulous antique place and an art studio that always showcased some lovely African American artwork. I bought two paintings and a Tiffany lamp I was sure would look good in Room Seven.

By the time I pulled into my garage, I was beat, but my mood had lifted and I was ready to open up shop the next day and tackle the tasks at hand. But when I entered the front foyer, the hairs on the back of my neck stood up. I stood stock still, a bag in one hand and the paintings tucked under the other arm, my purse dangling from my right shoulder. The house was quiet, just as I'd left it. But something was wrong.

I felt it in my soul.

Leave, a voice in my head screamed, and since I'd never been in the business of arguing with that voice, which I knew as the Holy Spirit, I turned on my heels, dropped everything except my purse, and headed toward the door. Did I mention my age—sixty-two? Well, I moved as fast as I could, but my fast wasn't fast enough. I'd almost made it to the door when I felt something hit me in the back of the head. I felt myself fall right by the door, my head shouting with pain. I reached up to rub it as he stood over me, a young man I'd never seen before. He was holding a gun and yelling at me about the safe in my office with a panicked look on his face. I was scared, not necessarily of dying, but of leaving this world with unfinished business because I knew my work on this rock wasn't done.

I tried to answer and give him the combination, but my mouth wouldn't work. I closed my eyes, prayed to God that His will be done, managed to utter *Jesus*, and as suddenly as the young man appeared, he disappeared. I heard rapid footsteps and turned my head toward the open door where I could see him running down the alley of oaks. And that's the last thing I remember.

3
"Ain't it Strange"

Getting hit in the head wasn't nice. Finding out I had a concussion was even worse. Finding myself in a hospital bed was the pits. They said the mailman found me. Thank God for that. But according to the deputy who questioned me, they hadn't found the would-be burglar. Well, I suppose he was more than a would-be anything. According to that same deputy, who was also a member of my church, my computer and petty cash box were missing. He'd broken in through a patio door. I hadn't thought to set the alarm that day.

I was just grateful that The Lord spared me, and I was determined to do the things I knew I needed to do. Seeing a gun in your face has a way of making you see life for what it is—a flower that blooms and then quickly withers away. I had to make some stuff happen before I withered away.

What bothered me about the whole ordeal, though, was that the burglar was black. I had done so much for my community, built the manor up to what it was just for black folks. I'd grown up around and been the victim of enough racism in my lifetime to fill an entire volume of encyclopedias. And for one of my own people to see fit to rob me hurt me to my core. The manor was supposed to be a haven for us and one of us had tried to ruin that.

Well, all I could say was thank God for insurance, and I vowed to never leave without engaging the alarm system again.

***

Dee Dee had the biggest mouth in Holiness County. As soon as she got wind of me being in the hospital, she called my son, so I woke up the second morning of my hospitalization to find Man sitting next to my bed. He was slumped over, fast asleep, looking like I cut him from a pattern of his father. He was just as handsome as that man but had a heart and morals ten sizes larger than his, and I hated to worry him and take him away from his life in Florida. Then there was the fact that he'd already been pushing me to sell the manor and move closer to him. This little incident would only be fuel for his fire.

I sighed, decided to get this little confrontation over with. "Man... Man, wake up."

He snapped to attention. Man was in the service for a few years, said he'd learned to sleep lightly as a result. "Mama... you okay?"

I nodded. "I'm fine. Kind of had a feeling something was coming. You know God don't let nothing sneak up on me. Just didn't know it'd be me getting busted upside my head."

He stood and leaned in closer to me. "Mama, you're not going back there. It's not safe and—"

"Now look, in all the years I've been back here, nothing like this has happened before and I'm not letting this run me away from my dream home—the home you bought for me. Now, love got me that place and love is what keeps it open."

"Well, I'm staying for a while. We're gonna figure out something to make you safer. *Something.* If anything happened to you..."

I reached up and rubbed the stubble on his cheek. "I ain't going nowhere until God says different."

4
"Welcome Home"

When they finally released me, three days of poking and prodding had passed and I was more than ready to go home. Man drove me, reminding me along the way that he'd be staying for a while to help me get back on my feet and assist me with running the manor. I wanted to protest, but truth is, I was glad he was staying. He was my only child and only family. I'd spent so many years with him, raising him alone. Before he grew up, he was my world and we were very close. I missed him being my constant companion sometimes.

He made his living off of investments. Sometimes I thought he was kind of reckless with some of his investments, but what I saw as recklessness was actually shrewdness. He'd made a lot of money over the years, enough to buy the manor and gift it to me and to send me money every month to help keep the place afloat. I was blessed to have a son like him.

He parked his rental in front of the house, and as he helped me out of the car, I said, "We should've gotten something to eat on the way here. Dorcas is off on some pre-wedding trip with Farris, and I'm too weak to cook."

"I could cook," he said as he helped me negotiate the front steps.

"Sugar, I don't think there are any of those Ramen noodles in the kitchen."

He stopped at the door and I handed him the key. "You tryna say that's all I can cook?"

"That's all I've ever seen you cook. And if you're referring to heating up take-out in a microwave, that's not cooking, son. You need to find you a wife. And I'm the only old woman I know who doesn't have grandkids. I'm overdue. You're forty years old; you need to hop to it."

He groaned. "Don't start that again, Mama. I haven't found Mrs. Right, yet."

"Mm-hmm. From what I've seen, you've been too busy with all those Mrs. Wrongs. Mrs. Right doesn't stand a chance with you."

As soon as we entered the foyer, a heavenly aroma infiltrated my nose.

"Well, smells like we don't need to worry about my cooking skills today," he said.

I smiled. "Is Dorcas here?"

"No, Ms. Dorcas ain't the only person in the world who can cook," Dee Dee said as she appeared in the foyer. She gently embraced me and added, "I'm glad you're okay, Ms. Rosa."

"Me, too, sugar."

"I called Rochelle and August and Dorcas and told them what happened. They're all so upset they're not here and told me to tell you they'll be here at the drop of a hat if you need them."

"That's sweet of them but not necessary. What you cooking?" I asked.

"Whatever it is, it sure smells good," Man said.

I glanced at him to see him staring at Dee Dee with a look in his eyes I'd never seen before. When I returned my attention to Dee

Dee, she was blushing. *Oh, Lord*, I thought. If I had to choose a woman for my son, Dee Dee's crazy butt wouldn't be her.

"Uh, Dee Dee, I don't think you've ever met my son. The last time he was here was years ago, before I hired you. This is Man, and Man, this is Dee Dee Jones."

"Dionne Jones, actually," she corrected, as she offered Man her hand. "We've talked on the phone a few times over the years. Glad to finally meet you."

"Freeman Stark," he replied. "It's a pleasure to meet you."

Hmm, formal names. Okay. "Well, *Dionne* and *Freeman*, I'm ready to eat."

They snapped out of their mutual trances and Man escorted me to the dining room.

"What's she do around here, Mama?" Man asked once we settled at the table.

I looked up at him with a smirk on my face. "Why you whispering, boy?"

He raised his eyebrows and just stared at me.

Before I could answer, Dee Dee brought two plates heaping with bacon, scrambled eggs, huge homemade biscuits, grits with butter, and home fries.

After she left, I said, "She's the housekeeper."

Through a mouthful of food, Man said, "She needs to be the cook. Wow!"

As I dug in, I had to agree. The girl could cook. When she returned with two tall glasses of orange juice, Man's eyes followed her every move.

"This is good, Dee Dee. Why didn't you tell me you could cook?" I asked.

She shrugged. "I'm a black woman in the south. I figured you knew."

She returned to the kitchen, and I said, "She's got a boyfriend, Man."

"So she's not married? Good!"

I shook my head as I continued to enjoy my breakfast.

***

So much for Man helping me out. Seemed like the only thing he was doing was being all up in Dee Dee's face constantly. So I sat in my office, feeling a little light-headed as I sifted through the resumes and applications again. At least I'd found a replacement for Dorcas. No way was Dee Dee going to keep cleaning up when she could cook like she did that morning. But now I had to find a new housekeeper, and I still needed to replace Rochelle. And as soon as I got myself a computer to replace the one that was stolen, I would take care of some other pressing business with Man's help.

By lunchtime, I was famished and made my way to the dining room in anticipation of more of Dee Dee's culinary goodness. She was so happy when I offered her the new job, she'd probably cooked herself to death. Imagine my surprise when I entered the dining room to find her and Man locked in a kiss in a corner of the room. I cleared my throat as I took my seat. They broke apart and Man wore a sheepish expression as he took a seat across from me. *How did I not see this mess coming?* I wondered. *That blow to the head must've knocked me off of my game.*

"She have time to cook, or have you been distracting her?" I asked.

"She cooked," he said.

"Wipe your mouth, son. That shade of lipstick doesn't match your complexion."

He grinned as he wiped Dee Dee's lipstick from his mouth.

I rolled my eyes. "You need to stop fraternizing with my employee."

"Then you need to stop hiring such fine employees."

Lord, help me.

5
"Workin' Together"

The next morning, I felt a little better and I was sure being home had a lot to do with that. We were two weeks away from hosting a big event—Dorcas's wedding—and I was more determined than ever to finalize all of the arrangements and set up some interview appointments to replace my missing employees. I rose early, showered and dressed, and headed to Room Ten. I often said my morning prayers in that room when it wasn't occupied, because I could feel God's presence strongly there.

I used my master key, opened the door, and was greeted by a chorus of feminine and masculine moans and the image of my son's naked backside in motion. I frowned, and it took me a few seconds to fully realize what was going on. Evidently, it had been just that long for me, or maybe it was because this was my son and although he was a grown man, I'd never associated him with sex—*ever*. I knew he had it, had a trail of exes to prove it, but Lord knows I'd never witnessed him doing the deed. Furthermore, this was a sight I *never* wanted to see.

I shrieked, ducked back into the hall, and walked faster than I had in years away from that room.

"Mama!" I heard him yell from behind me, but I couldn't stop. I needed to get that image out of my head. If I wasn't taking pain pills off and on, I would've made a beeline for the sitting room and drank up as much liquor as possible.

"Ms. Rosa! I'm sorry!" That voice made me stop in the middle of the staircase. I turned around, steadied myself by grasping the banister, and saw Man standing there in his boxers. Standing next to him with a sheet wrapped around her body was Dee Dee.

"Dee Dee?!" I shouted.

"Yes, ma'am. I'm so sorry. It just... happened. I'ma clean the room up, though."

"Well, it didn't *just* happen. It kinda happened all night long," Man said with a grin.

Dee Dee giggled and slapped his arm.

I turned on my heels and continued down the stairs. Man quickly caught up with me and followed me into my office. "Mama—"

"Boy, have you lost your mind?! You just met her yesterday!"

"I know. I can't explain it. It's like we just... clicked."

"And y'all had to click in *that* room?"

"She picked the room."

"Humph, I bet she did."

"I think I'm falling in love with her, Mama. She's so sweet and funny. She's *everything*."

"Sweet Jesus."

"She's wonderful."

"Mm-hmm. Wait till she tells you about all of her cousins."

He frowned. "What?"

"Nothing. Go get dressed so you can come help me. There's a lot to do, and evidently, you've got too much time on your hands."

"Mama…"

I tilted my head to the side and gave him *the look.*

"Yes, ma'am. Be right back."

***

"How long are you gonna give me the silent treatment, Mama?"

I looked up at my son, who was sifting through the stack of resumes and applications for me, and sighed before returning my attention to the pile of paperwork in front of me.

"Really, Mama? You didn't talk to me or Dee Dee at breakfast, and we've been in here for over an hour now. This is ridiculous. You act like I killed someone or something."

I removed my eyeglasses and fixed my eyes on my only child, who was sitting on the opposite side of my desk in a chair so low his knees looked uncomfortably close to his chest. He'd inherited his height from his father. "Why don't you go grab you a chair from the dining room? That one looks uncomfortable."

"I'm fine in this chair. Talk to me, Mama," he pleaded.

Even at forty, he was still my baby boy, and I couldn't stand to hear him whine. "Freeman—"

"Oh, Lord, you called me Freeman…"

"You want me to talk, don't interrupt me."

He nodded in concession.

"Freeman, I know I was never married to your father or any of the other men in my life, but I also know I taught you better than to jump into bed with a woman hours after you've just met her. You are being reckless. You don't know Dee Dee like that. She's sweet in her own way, but she's in a relationship, has been for years as far as I know, and you don't want to get in the middle of that. Plus, if it doesn't work out between you two, I'm gonna have to deal with the fallout while you skip your merry little self back to Florida."

He leaned forward, settling his gaze on me. "I hear you, Mama. It was reckless of me—"

"And I hope you used protection. The last thing you need to do is make a baby with someone who isn't your wife. That's a recipe for disaster. What if she gets with another man and he mistreats your child? What can you do when you live states away?"

"Come on now, Mama. You think I'd be stupid enough to have unprotected sex with her? I lost my virginity a long time ago, have had plenty of sex, and have no kids or diseases."

I sighed again. "I just wanted better for you than what I had, son. Marriage, then the rest. Doing things out of order leads to nothing but trouble."

"Okay, I won't touch Dee Dee again until after I marry her."

"Marry her?!"

"See, it's not about doing things the right way. You just don't want me with her. Why? You think she's not good enough for your baby boy?"

"Man, look. You know that everyone who has worked for me has a past. Rochelle came to me broken, hurt, coming down from drugs, and pregnant. August came to me addicted and a hot mess. Dorcas was in a bad place mentally, having just lost her husband. And Dionne has a past, too. You should ask her about it."

"You talking about her going to jail for shoplifting years ago? She told me about that and that it's way in her past. I'm actually shocked you brought it up. You of all people know better than to judge people by their pasts."

I opened my mouth to respond but was interrupted by loud voices coming from the foyer. Man stood to investigate. I followed him to find the tall, statuesque Dee Dee and a short, scrawny-looking man in the middle of a heated argument.

"How you gon' break up with me in a text message, Dee Dee?! Huh?!" the man shouted.

"I ain't tryna fight with you, Hudson. It's over. Ain't nothing you can do or say to change that," Dee Dee said.

"Why? Is it about the job? I told you I can't deal with that job. They don't treat those chickens right, Dee!"

"It's always something, Hud! Look, it's over. Just get your things and go back to your mama's where I found you."

He moved closer to her, and Man stepped forward. "Hold on, player. You heard the lady. She said y'all are over," Man said.

Dee Dee's eyes shifted to Man, and she looked as if she was about to explode with adoration. This was all too much for me.

"Who are you?!" Hudson asked, turning to Dee Dee. "Dee, you got something going with him?"

"She does," Man said.

"We're in love," Dee Dee added.

I closed my eyes and shook my head.

"Love?! Dee! You cheated on me?"

"Don't matter. We were over a long time ago; I just couldn't face it."

"This how you wanna play it, Dee? Okay, well… me and your friend, Lawanna, been messing around for months now."

She rolled her neck and said, "Read my lips: I. Don't. Care. Boy, bye!"

Hudson's eyes shifted from Dee Dee to my son, who outsized him greatly, and then he turned and stormed out of the house.

"Lord, I hope that little man don't come back here and burn my house down," I said.

Dee Dee, who was now enclosed in Man's arms, said, "Hud ain't gon' do nothing. He's a bunch of talk, that's all."

"I hope you're right, sugar," I said.

Man held her tight and softly said, "You all right, baby?"

She smiled up at him and nodded, and I turned and walked back to my office to be with the only sane person left in Hyacinth Manor—me.

6
"Reason"

I stood in the sitting room staring out the patio doors as the groundskeeper tended to the dead grass in the backyard. Over the past days, I'd managed to finalize everything for Dorcas's wedding and had hired a cousin of Dee Dee's named Aaliyah to be the new housekeeper. She seemed nice and sane with good references, so I was hopeful she'd work out. When Man wasn't sniffing in behind Dee Dee, he helped by answering the phone and even updated my website. I hadn't caught him and Dee Dee into anything else, but I was still a little taken aback by their whole affair. Man was tall, muscular, had been a fitness buff for years. And he was as handsome as his daddy, who made heads turn everywhere he went. My boy was college educated and up until this point, very smart, disciplined, and calculated when it came to business.

Dee Dee, on the other hand, was tall, but shorter than Man, and wide and loud. Okay, she had a good body, there was just a lot of it. Her current hairstyle of choice was an electric blue wig, and she'd never finished high school. She was impulsive, too, and she was about ten years younger than Man. They were terribly mismatched, and it confused and concerned me. And once again, I didn't see the whole thing coming... at all. I was definitely losing my gift, and that concerned me, too.

But I had other things to worry about, including an assignment I'd been ignoring for a long time, and I was going to need my love-struck son to help me figure some stuff out. So I decided I was going to leave him and Dee Dee alone as long as their little love affair didn't interrupt the daily operation of my business at the manor or the hosting of my dear friend Dorcas's wedding.

After I declared a truce with Man, I nearly had to drag him away from the kitchen, where I found him perched on a stool watching Dee Dee cook, to my office. There, I explained what I needed him to do.

***

"Let me get this straight. You feel led to find a descendant of Richard and Essie? Why? Because of *that room*?"

"I don't know, Man. I just know it's something I need to do. I've been needing to do it for a long time but I'm not good with computers, especially this new-fangled one you went out and bought me to replace the other one. And don't say *that room* like that. I know you think the legend is just an old wives' tale, but one night in it with Dee Dee and you think you're instantly in love."

He shook his head. "How do you know I wouldn't have fallen in love with her without that room? I sure didn't need that room to know I liked what I saw. Still do."

I sighed. "Look, are you going to help me or not? I just need you to see if you can find a Jarsdel that links directly to Essie and Richard."

"And then what?"

"And then, I suppose the good Lord will tell me what to do."

"Okay. You found an assistant yet?"

"Why? You tired of helping me?"

"No, ma'am. I love being here."

"Mm-hmm. I'm sure you do."

He smiled. "I was just asking because I think you're making the search harder than it has to be."

"How so?"

"I was looking through your reject pile and you've got some good candidates in there, folks with lots of experience. You need to call some of them in for an interview."

"Why would I do that if I already decided they're rejects?"

"Because you need an assistant since your other one is married and gone. I don't see a thing wrong with half of the folks in that pile. What are you using for hiring criteria?"

"If they've been in jail or are white, I don't hire them," I said as I reclined in my chair at my desk.

He stood from where he'd been sitting on the edge of my desk. "Mama, you can't use race as hiring criteria. That's racist. If anyone finds out, they could sue you."

"How is anyone gonna find out?"

"You know what I mean. The whole invitation-only thing is bad enough, but I do understand why you don't want to serve white people here. It's wrong, but I understand it. But this makes no sense. I would think letting white people serve your guests would be right up your alley."

"I don't trust them and my mission is to help my *own* people."

"I know you're not saying God told you to only help black people."

"No, the fact that I'm a black woman and know that my people have always been three steps behind white folks told me that. Look, you just help me find what I'm looking for and don't worry about how I choose to run my business."

He sighed as he logged onto the computer. "Yes, ma'am."

7
"Timin'"

"*You* already found them?" I asked. I was in my room, digging through my closet trying to find my gold shoes for Dorcas's wedding, which was in a week. She and her fiancé, Farris, were back in town, but I'd told her not to worry about returning to work since Dee Dee was doing a great job with the cooking. So was my new housekeeper, and Man had proven to be invaluable help to me. We only had one guest, and as we prepared for the nuptials, everything was going smoothly.

"Yes, ma'am. I found some good information on a website dedicated to Richard and Essie."

I turned and looked at him as he sat on the foot of my bed with my new laptop. "Well, don't just sit there. What'd you find?"

"Well, evidently, Essie kept a diary and someone scanned the pages and put them on the site. You should read them."

"Okay..."

"After they moved to New York, they had three kids, Richard, Jr., Emily, and Sarah."

I felt a little tug on my heart at the thought of three children created by their love, took a seat at my dressing table.

"Sarah passed away at a young age," he continued.

I gasped.

"But Richard, Jr. and Emily grew into adulthood and eventually had their own kids. They both married black people. But before any of that, shortly after Sarah, the youngest, died, Richard returned home to Arkansas for the first time to attend his father's funeral. Of course it was too dangerous for Essie and the kids to accompany him. So they stayed behind."

I nodded. "Yes, of course."

"She wrote about how lonely she was without him and the joy of their reunion when he returned home. From what I read, they really loved each other and were very happy. Richard took good care of his family for as long as he could."

"For as long as he could?"

"A few years after his father died, his mother took ill and sent word for him to come back to Arkansas. He left again amid great protest from Essie. She wrote that she knew something bad would happen if he returned home again, but this was his mother and he felt obligated to see about her as he was his parents' only child. He was only able to spend a week with his mother before she died of some type of fever. He buried her and locked this old place up, and by the time he returned to New York, he was showing signs of the fever that took his mother. A few days later, he died in Essie's arms, leaving her and their two teenaged kids to fend for themselves."

I felt tears fill my eyes. All this time, their story had felt like a fairy tale to me. Now that I'd heard the continuation, my heart broke for Richard and Essie.

"Essie and the kids managed to make do, but she never married again and died at a ripe old age. As I said before, the kids married black people, although Essie wrote in her diary about her desire for them to marry white people so that their children would have easier lives."

I frowned. "Really?"

"Yep. Anyway, I dug around and found out the site is maintained by one of the descendants of Richard, Jr., a Laura Thomas. She lives in Buffalo, New York."

I leaned forward. "You find her contact information?"

"Yeah, but if you want to talk face to face with a descendant, I found her father's information, too, and he lives out in the county, about twenty minutes from here."

I shot to my feet. "What?!"

He handed me a piece of paper and I read it aloud, "*Dean Jarsdel, 22365 Highway 126. 65 years old. Retired military.*" I looked up at Man and thanked him. And then I grabbed my purse and headed out of my room.

"Where you going, Mama?"

"To see Mr. Dean Jarsdel."

"Wait, let me go with you. You shouldn't be going out there alone."

"He's sixty-five. I'll be fine. Anyway, I think this is something I need to do alone."

***

I pulled into the white-washed driveway of a neat brick house situated on the side of the highway and turned my car off. My hand shook as I pulled the key from the ignition. I was so close to meeting a direct descendant of Essie Jarsdel that I could just taste it. It was surreal and exciting. My stomach was in knots as I closed my eyes and whispered a prayer to God: "Dear Lord, I don't know why I'm here, but You do. Please give me the words to say and show me Your true assignment for me. In Jesus' name, amen."

I opened my eyes and noticed someone sitting on the porch that had been empty just seconds earlier. I adjusted my glasses and leaned closer to the windshield. Then I climbed out of my car and took a few steps to get a closer look. It was him, all right. I'd know that face anywhere. "Hey!" I yelled.

The young man, the same one who'd robbed and assaulted me, sprung to his feet and took off running in the direction of the thick woods behind the house.

I walked around the house, my eyes searching for the young man. What was *he* doing there? Had he hurt Mr. Jarsdel? As I made it to the back of the house, the undeniable scent of fish hit me, and a voice said, "You the one he's running from?"

I turned to see a man, a white man, a *shirtless* white man with rippling muscles and gray hair and a gray beard, seated at a wooden table with a bucket of fish at his feet. My breath caught in my throat for a second as confusion filled me, but not just from the fish smell. Who was this white man and why couldn't I stop looking at his muscles? "Uh... yes. He... he robbed my-me-my business."

He cut what looked like a brim open and began to remove its entrails, swore under his breath.

I turned my head.

"Hmm, I'm not surprised. That boy is walking trouble, always into something."

"I'm, uh, here to see a Mr. Dean Jarsdel. Is he okay? Is he related to that young man?"

The man wiped his hands on a towel and stood from his seat, making his way to me. He stood right in front of me, a few inches taller than me, and said, "I'm Dean Jarsdel, and that boy is my grandson."

8
"Feel That You're Feelin'"

I should have told him my name and why I was there. I should have called the police and told them I'd found the thief. I should have done *something*, but I couldn't do anything but stand there in utter and complete shock. I didn't expect for him to be white. I didn't expect that at all, and at the same time, I wasn't sure why it was such a shock. Living in this country, he could've been any color. I also wasn't expecting a sixty-five-year-old man to look like he looked—built and tall and Richard Gere handsome and... *sexy*. And when did I start seeing any white man as sexy?

So I just stood there with my mouth hung open.

He gave me a curious look and said, "Ma'am? Ma'am, are you okay?"

I wasn't sure if something was said between that and his introduction. I wasn't sure of anything but the fact that I needed to get the heck out of Dodge. So I turned and walked as fast as I could on my now rubbery legs. I could hear him following me and saying something, but my ears were filled with the whooshing sound of my own heartbeat, so I haven't a clue what he said.

I yanked my car door open, fell into my seat, and slammed the door in his face. Then I took a couple of deep breaths, opened the door again, and said, "I'm sorry. I shouldn't have come here."

Just as he said, "Ma'am," I shut the door in his face again and screeched out of his driveway.

Once home, I rushed to my bedroom and grabbed my laptop. One thing I knew how to do well on that thing was use YouTube. I'd mostly been watching a lot of old soul performances on that thing, but this time I searched for something else, something that would help me settle my mind. No, something that would help me find my mind again, because I figured I must've lost it when that boy knocked me upside my head, the way I was lusting after that white man.

I spent some time watching Brother Malcolm X speak the truth about everything I already knew to be true. Then I watched a documentary about the mass incarceration of black men. Then I pulled out my copy of Claudia Rankine's *Citizen: An American Lyric* and read for a while. Then I watched my DVD of *The Butler*. Then I listened to Nina Simone's "Young, Gifted, and Black" five times.

I was quiet over dinner, told Man everything went fine when he asked about the visit. But when I went to bed, my mind was filled with thoughts of Dean Jarsdel, a symbol of my people's oppressor—thoughts about his body. And evidently, *my* body was thinking about him, too.

***

I woke up the next morning feeling conflicted. I had lost my gift of discernment and second sight and my understanding of what it meant to be black. And in losing all of that, I had lost who I was.

Rosa Stark was a woman of color who loved men of color and worked hard to help other people of color. Rosa Stark had been with and known some of the most intelligent black men in the world. During my time away from Arkansas, I had attended parties and gatherings where I rubbed elbows with Cornel West and Al Sharpton and so many others.

Before I was a mother or a college graduate or a teacher or a business owner, I was a black woman. That was my identity, and in my mind, God made me for a black man. And though I hadn't found my black man soul mate yet, I knew he was still out there.

I walked into Room Ten and fell to my knees in the middle of the floor and begged God to give me my mind and my gifts back. I begged Him to make me Rosa Stark again and to make this strange woman, this race traitor who'd inhabited my body and infiltrated my life, leave. Then I stood, grabbed a blanket, and headed outside to sit on the front porch, hoping the crisp air would help me clear my head.

I sat on one of the padded benches that flanked the front door and stared out at my property. I loved my place, wasn't a day that passed that I didn't thank God for it or the people who had passed through my doors. I had met so many beautiful spirits, seen love blossom for many of them, hosted weddings for a few. I closed my eyes and smiled at the thought of my friend Dorcas's wedding. She'd survived so much—birthing and raising six kids, the death of her husband, a bout with cancer—she deserved the happiness Farris Kenwood had already pledged to give her. She'd worked hard all her life, had the achy joints to prove it, and if anyone deserved a good life, she did.

I opened my eyes to see an older model pickup truck ambling up the driveway, shaded by the alley of oaks as it made its way to the house. I knew that either it was someone looking for lodging, someone who just wanted to peep inside the historical old house, or someone needing directions. I plastered a smile on my face that I quickly dropped when the doors to the truck opened and my robber and his grandfather stepped out onto the driveway. I didn't stand, but watched as they approached the house, stopping before reaching the bottom of the front steps.

Dean Jarsdel wore a smile along with blue jeans and a flannel shirt with a baseball cap covering his thick hair. On his feet, he wore what looked to be steel-toe boots. His grandson wore blue jeans, a gray hoodie, and a dejected expression on his face.

"Hello, ma'am," the older man said.

Since my mind was clear, I noticed the deep twangy baritone of his voice and it played like music in my ears. *I like black men, no... I love them. I love their big juicy lips. I love everything about them,* I silently told myself. I nodded. "Um, how did you find me?" I asked and then told myself I should've apologized for popping up at his house and then running away like a mad woman and then I asked myself why I cared what this man thought of me.

"My grandson here knows the place well, I believe," Dean Jarsdel said, still wearing that smile. "Right, Julian?"

The young man nodded with his eyes downcast.

"*Right*, Julian?" his grandfather repeated, his voice much sterner this time.

Julian lifted his eyes and said, "Yes, sir."

"Ma'am—what's your name, ma'am?"

I hesitated before saying, "Ms. Stark."

"Well, Ms. Stark, Julian here has something to say to you."

The young man looked at me and stepped forward a few paces, stopping at the bottom of the steps. "I'm sorry, Ms. Stark, for breaking into your place and stealing from you. I... I..." He dug into the front pocket of his hoodie and pulled out a wad of money. "This is not all of your money, but as soon as I get a job, I'ma pay the rest." He rushed up the steps and handed the money to me and then hurried back to his spot on the driveway.

I looked at the young man—curly black hair, fair brown skin. He was handsome and there was something about him that told me that under the right circumstances, he could be someone great one day. "What about my computer?" I asked.

Dean Jarsdel looked shocked but didn't say anything.

Julian said, "I pawned it, but—" He looked over at his grandfather. "But I promise I'll get you another one."

"Mm-hmm. What do you have to say about hitting me?"

His grandfather nearly lost it then. "You hit her?! You hit a *woman*, Julian?!"

"Y-yes, sir," Julian stammered.

The older man stared at him for a second before turning to me. "Ma'am—Ms. Starks, I am embarrassed that I share blood with him right at this moment. I don't know what could've possessed him to do something like this, but rest assured, I will make sure he makes restitution to you even if it takes him the rest of his life. Right, Julian?"

Julian nodded. "Yes, sir."

"Tell *her*, not me!"

"Yes, ma'am."

"Get in the truck, Julian."

As Julian climbed into the truck and closed the door, his grandfather ascended the steps and stood right in front of me. "Ms. Stark, I want to offer my deepest personal apology for Julian's behavior. He's been known to get into trouble, but I've never known him to be violent. I wish there was someone else I could blame this on, some influence or peer pressure—anything—but as far as I know, he's a loner. I'm trying to help his mother with him since his father has passed on, but it seems I'm failing, and I'm failing badly."

I shook my head. "Don't blame yourself. One thing I know about children is that they have free will just like us adults. As hard as we try to mold them, it's still up to them to choose between right and wrong."

He nodded to the empty cushion next to me. "May I?"

I wanted to say no, but "sure" fell out of my mouth before I could stop it. He sat down beside me and suddenly the right side of my body felt warm. His body heat was better than any blanket, and Lord, he smelled so good!

He turned to me and said, "If you wanna call the police or press charges, I wouldn't blame you a bit, although I hope you do neither. I'd hate for him to have a rap sheet at his age."

"How old is he?" I asked, trying to ignore the thudding of my heart. He was too close and it was effecting my thinking.

"Eighteen."

"That's a hard age, a time of great transition. He's kind of straddling childhood and adulthood. Well, I know how it is to be young and confused and to make unwise decisions, and I don't believe anyone benefits from prison, so I won't be alerting the authorities of his identity."

"Thank you. Now, was that all you wanted when you came to my place the other day?"

No, I came to see you. "Uh-um, yes. That was it."

He stood. "Good. Well, you take care, Ms. Stark."

"Thank you. You do the same, Mr. Jarsdel."

I watched them leave and kind of wished they'd stayed.

9
"Love Is The Key"

The ballroom at my beloved Hyacinth Manor was draped in shades of cream and gold—Dorcas's favorite colors. Tables covered with gold tablecloths were situated on either side of an aisle which was lined with clear track lighting and cream-colored roses. The same roses served as centerpieces on the tables and adorned the arch that sat at the end of the aisle. After I surveyed the area and was satisfied that everything looked absolutely perfect, I returned to Room Ten where Dorcas was preparing herself for her groom.

I smiled as I entered the room. It felt like old times to see a glowing Rochelle sitting at the foot of the bed, smiling and chatting with Dee Dee, who was working on Dorcas's make-up. August's wife, Von, was sitting on the sofa, gazing up at her husband's brilliant artwork which hung over the fireplace, her belly round and full.

"I still can't believe you and August didn't tell me you were expecting," I said as I took a seat next to her with a soft grunt.

"We wanted to surprise you, Ms. Rosa," she said as she rested her hand on her belly.

"Well, that you did! I'm so happy for you two! And you both look so good," I said. And they did with coordinating outfits of cream and gold to match the event's color scheme.

"Well, you look just as elegant as you always do, Ms. Rosa," she replied.

"Thanks, sugar. Rochelle, how's married life treating to you?" I asked, turning my attention to the woman who'd been more of a daughter and friend to me than an employee.

"How does it look like it's treating me? Done gained ten pounds from all of the easy living I've been doing and T acts like he loves me more because of it, can't keep his hands off of me!"

I chuckled. "Well, I don't doubt that he loves you. I saw that written all over him the first day I met him."

"Hear you tell it, you always see everything a mile away," Rochelle said.

"She does!" Dorcas said as Dee Dee brushed eyeshadow onto her right eyelid. "She told me Farris was gonna come courting months before it happened. I didn't believe it."

"Hmmm, that's funny," Dee Dee said.

"What is?" Dorcas asked, sounding a little insulted.

"Oh, not you and Mr. Farris. I was just thinking; all these married and finna be married folk in this room, and Von is the only one who stayed in here."

"You're forgetting about yourself, aren't you?" I asked.

Dee Dee blushed and was bombarded with questions from the other ladies. She shook her head. "I don't want to talk about it." She glanced up at me with shame in her eyes and I felt a little tug on my heart.

Rochelle raised her hand. "I spent a night in here, too, once. When you were out of town, Rosa."

My mouth dropped open.

Dee Dee said, "I knew it!"

"Lord, I might as well tell the truth. I spent about three nights in here," Dorcas said.

I gasped.

"Ms. Dorcas!" Dee Dee shrieked.

"Girl, I was tired of Farris dragging his feet."

"How did I miss all of this under my own roof?" I asked.

"You're slipping, Ms. Rosa," Rochelle said. The other ladies burst into laughter. They had no idea how close she was to the truth.

***

Watching my dear friend exchange vows with a man whose love for her was as obvious as the nose on anyone's face was beautiful and touching, and more than one time, I found myself wiping tears and noticed many others doing the same thing as the couple recited their own vows, declaring an eternal love for one another. The highlight of the ceremony for me was watching Dorcas's four sons, who all towered over her petite frame, escort her down the aisle and give her to her groom. Her oldest son, Kevin, shook Farris's hand and said, "You better take care of my mama," with tears in his eyes and a shaky voice. I don't think there was a dry eye in the place after that.

Their beautiful wedding took my mind back to a time when I was young and wanted to be in love. I had foolishly thought Man's father could be the one, but at the end of the day, he wasn't, and looking back on it, his being a married man should've cancelled him out in my mind anyway. After that relationship turned my life upside down, I was more cautious about the male company I kept.

Other men came and went—handsome men, rich men, nice men, blue collar men. Many gave me expensive gifts, took me on trips, even proposed marriage, but none of them made my pulse race or my head spin. Although they professed their love for me, I never felt the same for them, and by the time I returned to Arkansas some sixteen years ago, I was convinced I would never and could never fall in love. If I couldn't love those good men from my past, how could I possibly love any man? And I was fine with that, had accepted my permanent state of single-ness, and was happy living alone and on my own. I had my manor employees, who were the closest thing I had to family besides Man, since all of the other family I knew of was gone on to glory, and even though Dorcas was older than me and Rochelle and August were more the age younger siblings would be than offspring, I felt like they were all my children and my nest was emptying. Everyone was finding love and moving away, and looking at Man and Dee Dee as they snuggled closely together at their table, I feared they would be next, leaving me totally alone to hire strangers in hopes of them becoming family to me, too. I didn't want to be alone, and suddenly, being perpetually single wasn't appealing to me and was beginning to make me feel like something was wrong with me. What in my brain and heart had always prevented me from falling in love? I wished I knew and I wished I could fix it.

As the preacher said, "I now pronounce you man and wife," I stood with everyone else in the ballroom and cheered and applauded with tears racing down my cheeks.

10
"Family"

After seeing Dorcas and Farris off, I joined my manor family in the ballroom where we were the only people left of the attendees. We all gathered around one table, laughing and talking, devouring leftover food and polishing off what remained of the champagne. Rochelle's husband, the one and only Teo B, blessed us with a few of his hits performed a cappella, and once he finished singing the fourth love song, he and Rochelle excused themselves to their room. It was a good thing their son had already left with his grandparents, because from the look in Rochelle's eyes, Teo was in for a treat.

August, in his own soft-spoken way, told us about his and Von's travels and about how excited they were about the later-in-life baby they were expecting.

Dee Dee and Man were in a world of their own, gazing into each other's eyes, grinning and giggling. And there I sat in the midst of it all, amongst family but alone. When the doorbell chimed throughout the house, I welcomed the opportunity to leave the table for a moment, but Man stopped me as I stood to answer it. "I'll get it, Mama. Probably one of the guests who left something behind. That champagne'll make you forget things." He winked at Dee Dee, who giggled and lifted her glass.

"While he's checking the door, I'm going to the little girl's room," I said to no one in particular.

I left and had almost made it to the closest bathroom when I heard someone call my name. "Ms. Rosa! Wait!"

It was Dee Dee. I turned and watched as she approached me with a timid expression on her face. She looked nice in her gold dress. She'd taken her heels off and padded toward me in bare feet.

"Ms. Rosa. I just wanted to say that I really do care for Freeman, but I've noticed that you haven't had much to say to me since you found out about us. Ms. Rosa, you mean the world to me, hired me five years ago when no one else in this little town would, put up with my crazy mouth. If being with your son means I can't have you in my life, then I'll break things off with him right now. I love him, I really do, but I've known and loved you longer. My mama is gone. You're the only mama I have left."

I felt like what I had been acting like—a butthole—as I tilted my head to the side, blinked back tears, and cradled her face in my hands. "I just want you to be happy. I want my boy to be happy, too, and if you two make each other happy, then I have no problem with you being together." And I meant every word. After all, who was I to judge anyone?

She grabbed me and pulled me into a hug. "Thank you, because as my cousin Aretha would say, he makes me feel like a natural woman!"

I stepped out of the hug and patted her shoulder. "I don't need details, sugar."

After standing in the bathroom and staring at my reflection in the mirror for five or ten minutes, as if I could stare the lines on my face and the gray that was overtaking my hair away, I finally washed and dried my hands. Don't get me wrong, I looked good and I knew it; never had I doubted that. Never did I think I was anything less than a black queen. I was just... *tired*.

A soft knock came at the bathroom door. "Mama?" Man's voice penetrated the wood of the door and floated into my ears.

I opened it and gave him a slight frown. "Was I in here so long they sent you to get me?"

He shook his head. "No, ma'am. The door was for you. There's someone waiting to see you."

"Who?"

Man shrugged. "Never seen him before."

I brushed my hands over the front of my cream empire-waist dress, glanced down at my pink house shoes, and shrugged. Once I made it into the foyer, I stopped dead in my tracks. His back was turned to me but I knew it was him. He was wearing blue jeans and a plaid long-sleeve shirt. No cap covered his hair this time.

"Um, Mr. Jarsdel?" I said.

He spun around with a smile on his face which quickly faded away. "Um-uh-um, M-Ms.-Ms..."

"Stark."

"Ms. Stark, yeah, that's right." He ran his fingers through his hair and gave me a nervous smile. "You... you look beautiful. If I'd known better, I would've dressed up, too."

I glanced down at myself. "Oh, thank... thank you. We just hosted a wedding. Things are winding down now."

He smiled and nodded.

I just stood there until I finally thought to say, "Um, is there something I can help you with?"

His face lit up. "Yes, um, do you like fish?"

"Fish? Yes, why?"

"Well, I got a mess of brim and crappies, all cleaned and frozen. I was over this way and decided to drop by and see if you wanted some."

"Uh... Well..."

"Shoot, yeah, she wants some!" Man said. I didn't realize he was a few steps behind me.

Dean Jarsdel looked at my son, then at me.

"Sure. Bring them by anytime," I said against my will.

"It'll be sooner rather than later," Dean said.

I gave Man the evil eye after Dean Jarsdel was safely in his truck.

"What?" he asked. "So, you don't like fish?"

"That's not the point."

"What's the point? That you found the descendent and he's white? You weren't gonna tell me that, huh?"

"It wasn't important."

"He likes you."

"What? No, he doesn't."

"Yes, he does. For all of your talk about discernment and gifts, you couldn't discern that man making googly eyes at you?"

I swatted him on the arm and then made my way back to the ballroom.

***

He wasn't kidding when he said it'd be sooner rather than later. I'd barely finished my breakfast the next day when Dean Jarsdel arrived with a cooler full of fish and a gallon-sized Ziploc bag full of crawfish for good measure. I stood on the front porch and watched in awe as Man and August unloaded the food from the back of his pickup. "Uh... thank you," I yelled from my vantage point.

Mr. Jarsdel took off his ball cap and nodded. "Most welcome, Ms. Stark," he said and then began to ascend the steps, and I suddenly became a bundle of nerves. I backed into the bench and sat down.

When he was finally standing directly in front of me, I blurted, "I appreciate your kindness, but I already told you I won't press charges against your grandson, so there's no need for you to do anything like this again."

His eyes, which I had just at that moment realized were green, *emerald* green, widened. "Oh, no, ma'am. That wasn't my intention. I fully believe you are a woman of your word. I fish a lot. Love to fish, actually, and I don't have many friends around who like to catch or eat fish as much as I do. I just like to share, hate for them to go to waste."

"You don't have any family around?"

"Other than Julian, no. My daughter's in the east. My son's in Iowa."

"Your son?"

"Yes. Brandon. He's single, though, no kids. Julian's my only grandchild."

"I see." I crossed my legs, noticed his eyes dart to them then back to my face, and thought that maybe Man was right about him liking me. Then I chased that thought away because there was no way I could like him back. "How *is* Julian?"

He sighed. "I don't know. Losing his father has been hard for him and I know I can't replace him. His father was some kind of man. Loved his family and worked hard to take care of them."

I nodded.

We were silent, our eyes on each other, off of each other, then on each other again. He was handsome. He had a nice body. His eyes were piercing. His voice was nice, and he seemed kind. All of that I could admit. But being around him made me feel strange, like my insides were constantly swelling and about to explode. And I was so darn jittery. Lord, what was going on with me?

"Well, I guess I'll let you go. See you at the fish fry tomorrow," he finally said.

"What?" If I'd been eating or drinking I'd have surely choked to death right then and there.

"Your son invited me—I think he's your son, right? Big, tall?"

"Freeman?"

"Yes, Freeman, that's right. I told him I can make a mean coleslaw. Old family recipe. I'll bring it. See you later, Ms. Stark."

I didn't give him a chance to even make it to the bottom step before I stormed inside to find Man in the kitchen all hugged up with Dee Dee, the huge ice chest sitting in the middle of the floor. "Have you lost your rabid mind, boy?!" I yelled, startling them both so that they sprung apart.

"Mama—what—"

"A fish fry? And you invited that white man to come?! Freeman

Martin Malcolm Stark, how dare you!"

"My *whole* name? Okay, look, he's got some black in him if he's Essie's great-great-great-great-great-great-great-whatever, right? That should count for something."

"Not enough black."

"Well, I invited him and I'm not *un*inviting him. I mean, he provided the fish; the least we can do is invite him to help eat it."

"We don't serve whites here, Man! And you know that!"

"You're a racist."

"No, I'm not! You obviously don't know the definition of that word if that's what you think I am."

"Then what do you call it, because it sure seems racist to me."

"I'm educated and liberated. And you know what? You can have your little fish fry, but I won't be there." And with that, I flounced out of the kitchen and strutted to my office.

11
"Reachin' Down Inside"

The weather *would* be nice that day. Sixty-five degrees. The second cold snap lifted just for that day it seemed, and my plotting son took full advantage of it. He held his little fish fry out in the backyard, blasted Maze featuring Frankie Beverly music at the highest possible decibel. Teo and Rochelle and their son, Justin, were there. So were August and Von, and of course, Dee Dee. The way they were hooting and hollering, Man must've paid them to act like they were having the time of their lives in order to entice me into coming out of hiding. Well, he could just give that up.

I opened Hyacinth Manor with the intention of a white person never having the pleasure of being served there again and that was still my intention. Slaves had walked those halls and catered to the Jarsdels for years. Well, I wasn't a slave, and I wasn't about to cater to that man even if he did have one distant black relative. And why was he hanging around the manor so much, anyway? It just didn't set right with me.

My bedroom window was just over where Man set up his little shindig so I could hear them, but I couldn't see them. And though I had my old window closed, the smell of fried fish seemed to seep in through the cracks and crevices of the wooden window frame. I sat at my dressing table, scarf on my head, and listened to the muffled sounds of "Before I Let You Go," one of my favorite Maze songs, and tapped my foot to the rhythm. Then I heard a chant ring out: "Go, Dean! Go, Dean!"

I frowned, walked over to the window, and peered out of it for the tenth time. I still couldn't see anything but I had to admit that my interest was piqued. The song changed to "Back in Stride," and the chanting began again. I sat at the foot of my bed. I loved a good party, always had, and that son of mine knew it. And he also knew I was nosy, was probably leading that chant just to get my goat. He knew I'd want to see for myself just what Dean was doing.

He won.

I snatched the scarf off of my head, threw on a pair of jeans and a blouse, picked out my afro, decided to forgo makeup, and made my way out to the festivities. The couples were getting down. Dean was sitting at a table laughing, watching them.

I'd been duped.

Either that, or I'd missed his little dancing display, but I leaned more toward having been duped. I stood there by the patio doors wanting to put all of my guests out, and just as I turned to head back into the house, I felt a hand on my shoulder. "I was wondering if you were coming."

Twangy, baritone, *his* voice.

I turned and faced him, felt my stomach churn from more than the hunger the smell of the fried fish evoked. His face was inches from mine, his eyes glued to mine, and innately, I wanted to kiss him or for him to kiss me. "I..."

"Southern Girl" began to play, another favorite of mine. My eyes darted to the spot of grass everyone was using as a dancefloor. Dean reached for my hand. "You wanna dance, Ms. Stark?"

I did. I really did, but I shook my head and said, "No. I think I'll fix myself a plate."

"Take a seat. I'll fix you one."

Since my legs had suddenly turned into pepper jelly, I agreed and sat at one of the patio tables that I'd handpicked and bought shortly before opening for business. I sighed. My so-called friends and family waved at me, flashing conspiratorial smiles. I rolled my eyes.

"Here you go," Dean said as he placed the heaping plate before me. But when he sat down directly across from me, I felt my appetite leave.

"You can dance if you want. Don't let me stop you," I said.

He shook his head and smiled, his green eyes gleaming. "I'd rather dance with you."

I frowned slightly. "Why?"

"Because I've always loved dancing with pretty ladies."

I nearly dropped the piece of fish I was holding and thinking about attempting to eat. I felt my face heat up. "Uh... does your wife know you like to do that?"

"My *ex*-wife? Yes, she knows, probably doesn't care anymore."

I took a bite of fish, chewed, and said, "Oh."

"You ever been married, Ms. Stark?"

"No," I said through a mouthful of coleslaw. It was delicious, but I couldn't bring myself to tell him.

"Ms. Stark, I'm sure you can tell that I'm very attracted to you."

I nearly spit out the soda I'd just sipped. "You're what-why?"

"I'm attracted to you, very, *very* attracted to you. Why? Because you're beautiful, kind, smart, *sexy*… everything I like in a woman."

"Mr—"

"Please call me Dean."

"Um, Dean, I'm-I'm flattered, I really am, but—"

"I know I look kind of like a redneck, but I'm not. I'm retired Navy. I love people, I love my family, I love to have a good time, and I'd love to get to know you."

"Uh…"

"You are truly a beautiful woman, you know that?"

"I—thank you—please excuse me." I stood from the table in haste, knocking my chair over in the process, and I left that little party and didn't return.

***

I was sitting at my desk a couple of days later when a knock came at the door. I looked up to see a crowd entering my office—Rochelle, Dee Dee, August, Von, and Man. "No Teo?" I asked.

"He and Justin are packing up the car. We gotta get him back to school, and T needs to get back to finish up his new album," Rochelle said.

"Oh, I didn't realize y'all were leaving so soon. But does everyone have to say goodbye in here?"

"That's not why we're here, Ms. Rosa," August said.

"Is something wrong?" I asked, my eyes shifting from person to person.

"We need to talk to you about your behavior," Man said.

"What? Are y'all crazy? My behavior? I'm growner than all of y'all!"

"Ms. Rosa, it's a shame the way you treated that nice Mr. Dean," Dee Dee said. "Nice, fine Mr. Dean," she added softly.

I shook my head and leaned against the back of my chair. "You need to take that up with Man. You know I don't serve white folks around here. Never have and never will."

"As far as I could see, he was the one serving *you*. He fixed *your* plate, Mama. He also fixed his own plate," Man said.

Von nodded. "And he got me seconds, too."

"He's a sweet man. Broke my heart to see him sitting there waiting for you after you disappeared," Rochelle said.

"This is not any of y'all's business," was all I could think to say.

"Yes, it is. You're our family and we love you," Rochelle said. "And if you don't stop acting like this, Dean is going to slip through your fingers. I fought Teo with everything in me, but that man loves me more than he ever hurt me. I almost missed out on that, and let me tell you about the sex—"

"Please don't," August said. "You're like a sister to me. I don't wanna hear that."

Rochelle huffed and placed her hands on her hips. "Anyway, I almost missed out on a good life with all kinds of good loving in it," she said, cutting her eyes at August.

August sighed.

"Your situation is different, Rochelle," I replied.

Rochelle nodded. "Yeah, because Dean never hurt you. You are just holding his race—something that he can't even help—against him. And what's so crazy is you like him, too. We can all see that. You're just fighting it."

"You go to church, read the Bible, pray, and say you can read people, but you can't see that your thinking is wrong or that you belong with that man. Something isn't right about that, Ms. Rosa. You can't love Jesus and hate your fellow man," August said.

"You need to straighten up your act before you end up alone forever," Man interjected.

I opened my mouth to respond, but the very pregnant Von interrupted me. "You once told me that you knew I was August's, well somehow I know you're Dean's. Don't let pride or prejudice steal him away from you."

"And let's not forget that the man is fine, the finest old white man I think I've ever seen," Dee Dee said.

Then they all left me alone, and I couldn't concentrate for the rest of the day.

***

August and Von left the next morning. I gave Dee Dee the day off, so she and Man took a trip to Little Rock. And since there were no guests checked into the manor, I took the day off, too, to rest and try to gather my thoughts. Their little intervention had gotten to me. If you want to hurt my feelings, insult my gifts and my Christianity. They'd done both. And to make matters worse, they were right. I'd let my passion for my people override what it meant to truly be a Christian, and I had behaved horribly toward Dean Jarsdel when he'd been nothing but kind to me. I needed to make things right and apologize whether I liked him or not.

So I climbed into my car and drove to his roadside home. Knocked on the door and held my breath. It was Julian who opened it. His eyes widened when he saw me.

"Hi, Julian. Is your grandfather home?"

"Yes, ma'am… he's taking a nap."

My spirits fell a little. "Oh… well, tell him I dropped by. I'll come another time."

"No, ma'am. Come on in. He won't mind me waking him up for you."

I blushed a little at that statement. Had he been talking about me?

I walked inside the cozy home and sat on the plaid couch. It looked as one would expect a man's house to look—sturdy furniture, a huge TV, not spic and span, but neat enough. Pictures of people I assumed were family members crowded the end tables and hung on the walls. The scent of fried food seemed to have been absorbed into the walls.

I sat and folded my hands in my lap and fixed my eyes on the TV screen as I waited. *SportsCenter* was on. That was one of Man's favorite shows. I didn't particularly like sports, but I did a good job of appearing engrossed in the program.

"Ms. Stark!" He was shirtless again, wearing pajama bottoms, bed head, and a smile. And he was still handsome… and fine.

"Mr. Jarsdel."

"Dean."

"Dean, hi."

He plopped down in an easy chair and said, "What can I do for you today?"

"I'm sorry for waking you."

"No... no, I should've been up anyway."

"Um... Okay. I want—I *need* to apologize for my behavior the other day."

He shook his head. "No, I came on too strong. I'm the one who needs to apologize, Ms. Stark. That's always been a problem for me. I see something I want and I just... go for it."

I was supposed to say something else to him but my brain seemed to seize up at his last words.

"Where's my head? Would you like something to drink, Ms. Stark?"

"Yes, please. Thank you."

"Water, juice, soda?"

"Water is fine."

He left and I took a breath, tried to settle my nerves. When he returned and handed me the glass, our fingers touched. I gulped the water down and had to gasp for air. "You were saying?" I said breathily.

He grabbed an ottoman and placed it by my feet, sat on it, and reached for my hand. I gave it to him, felt sparks shoot up my arm, and wanted to snatch away from his grip. But I couldn't. I liked feeling the warmth of his calloused hand.

"I know I can be forward, but I can't help it sometimes. You are one beautiful woman. Beautiful and graceful. I just... I want to get to know you."

"Okay," I heard myself say.

"Really?"

I nodded.

"You mind if I kiss your cheek, Ms. Stark?"

"N-no, I don't mind."

I was trembling and the trembling only grew worse when his lips met my skin. "You cold, Ms. Stark?" he asked as he reached up and gently rubbed his hands up and down my arms.

I shook my head. "Just a little scared."

"Of me?"

"Yes," I whispered.

He cradled my face in his hands, his green eyes boring into my brown ones. "You don't have a thing to be scared of. I'm putty in your hands. I just want to spoil you, Ms. Stark. That's all."

I gave him a timid smile. "Since you're putty in my hands, I guess you should call me Rosa."

"What a beautiful name, almost as beautiful as you are."

"Thank you."

He stared at me for a moment before kissing me lightly on my lips. I closed my eyes, swooned a little, thought, *My Lord...*

"I forgot to ask for permission that time," he said, his mouth hovering near mine.

"It's-it's okay."

"Well, in that case..."

He rested his strong hands on my thighs and kissed me again. This time, I wrapped my arms around his neck and kissed him back, eager for more of his goodness. Then the sound of Julian clearing his throat shook us apart.

"Um…when's dinner, Grandpa?" he asked.

***

I stayed for dinner—fried pork chops, fried okra, and fried potatoes. I invited him to dinner at the manor the next day, because, although the man could cook and the food was good, I wanted to save my arteries.

That next evening, we ate with Man, who had a lively discussion with Dean as they compared military notes and traded service stories. After dinner, Dean joined me in the sitting room for drinks.

"This place is lovely, Rosa. I love what you've done with it."

"You've been here before?"

"Sure. When I first moved to Arkansas a few years ago. I'm sure you know this was the old Jarsdel plantation."

"Yes." I cringed at hearing the word *plantation*.

"I felt like I needed to see where my ancestors trod. But it's not a place or a part of my family's history that I'm proud of."

I nodded. "You know the story of Essie and Richard?"

"Yes, beautiful story, beautiful love."

"You come from their line?"

"Yes. I'm named after him. Dean is my middle name. My mother always called me Dean so it stuck."

"I see."

"You want to know why I'm white?"

"Um, I didn't say that."

He smiled. "You didn't have to. The bloodline got diluted, I guess. After Richard and Essie's kids, all of my ancestor's married whites. I suspect that has happened a lot in this country, white folks walking around with black blood in them. Some of them probably have no clue."

"That was what Essie wanted, to dilute the bloodline," I murmured.

"Yes. My daughter was the first in eons to marry a black person."

"How did you feel about that?"

"Like I said before, he was a good man. I loved him like a son rather than a son-in-law."

"Well, that's… wonderful."

"What's really on your mind, Rosa?"

"Just that you've enjoyed privilege because of your diluted bloodline, haven't you?" I hated that I'd said it, but I couldn't stop myself.

He gave me a thoughtful look. "I suppose so. That was what Essie wanted, too, I guess."

"I can see why she felt that way, but according to the one-drop rule, you're as black as I am."

He nodded. "True."

There was silence until his voice broke into it. With his drink in hand, he pointed a finger at me and said, "You don't like white people, do you?" as if it had just occurred to him.

"I never said that."

"But you don't, do you?"

I took a sip of my brandy. "To be honest, not particularly, no."

"Then you must be vexed about your feelings for me."

I opened my mouth to lie, decided against it.

"You dislike *all* white people?"

I nodded. "For the most part."

"Why? Did someone white hurt you?"

I scoffed. "I'm a black woman living in a patriarchal, white supremacist country. I grew up black, in Arkansas, in the fifties and sixties. My son's a black man. My ancestors were slaves. What do you think?"

"Did *I* ever hurt you?"

I frowned. "No."

"But my grandson did, right. My *black* grandson."

"Y-yes."

"And you forgive him, right?"

"Yes."

"Can you extend a little of that forgiveness toward me for being white?"

"How can I forgive you for being something you can't help?" I asked.

He smiled. "Exactly."

I sighed. "Okay, I see your point. I'm... I'm sorry."

"Can I see the room?"

"What room?"

"Richard's room that everyone at the fish fry told me about. The magic one."

I could've strangled those people, *my people*, if I didn't love them so much. I sat there for a moment before setting my drink down and standing to my feet. "Sure."

He followed me up the stairs and into Room Ten; I could feel his eyes on my body the whole way there and I liked the fact that he was appraising me, possibly craving what he saw. He walked into the room, turned in a slow circle as he took in his new surroundings. His eyes quickly settled on the painting over the fireplace, a showpiece of artwork I'd received as a gracious gift from August Donovan, who was an artistic savant of sorts.

"Beautiful," Dean softly said.

"Yes, it is."

"It's not you?"

"No, I don't know the model, but you've met the artist—August Donovan."

His eyes lit up. "Really? He is very talented. I wouldn't mind owning some of his work."

"I didn't know you were an art enthusiast."

He chuckled. "Can't tell by my house, huh?"

"Um… no. I can give you August's website address if you'd like."

"Yes, I'd appreciate that."

I took a seat on the sofa in the sitting area of the room as he stood in front of the painting, his attention fixed on it. "Can I ask you a question, Dean?"

He turned to face me, his hands in the pockets of his slacks. With his stiffly-starched dress shirt and slicked–down hair, he looked very nice. I liked the polished look on him. "Of course," he said.

"Have you always liked black women?"

He shrugged. "I suppose so. Never really thought about it. What I know for sure is that I've always liked beautiful women."

"But your wife was white."

"Yes... and beautiful. Almost as beautiful as you, Rosa."

I blushed. "You really should stop that."

"Why would I stop telling the truth?"

He sat down beside me and I cleared my throat. "But you've never dated a black woman before?"

"No. And you never dated a white man since you hate white people, right?"

"I don't hate white people. I hate what they've—what *many of them* have done to my people."

"So do I."

I nodded.

"So this is the room where people fall in love, huh?"

"I've found that to be the case. But the person has to spend the night in here."

He scooted so close to me that our thighs touched. "Have you ever spent the night in here, Rosa?"

"Huh? What?"

He smiled as his gaze dropped from my eyes to my lips. "Have you ever spent the night in here?"

"Y-yes." I couldn't believe I'd just admitted that.

"Hmm, I see."

I opened my mouth to explain, but almost instantly, he covered it with his and gave me a deep kiss tinged with liquor and full of more passion than I'd ever experienced in my life. I reached up and did something I'd been wanting to do since I met him. I dug my fingers in his thick silver hair as I kissed him back. He turned his head, deepened the kiss even though I didn't think that was possible.

He moaned softly.

So did I.

And if good sense hadn't kicked in, there's no telling how far things between us might have gone. I backed away from him and tried to catch my breath,

"Forgive me, but I couldn't help myself," he said. "I think it's going to be hard for me to control myself around you."

"It's going to be hard for me, too," I said barely above a whisper.

"Rosa—"

"Dean—"

We called each other's names in unison and then we both laughed. "You go first," he said.

"No, you."

"Rosa, can we give it a go? I want to see you exclusively. I want to be yours and I want you to be mine."

"You do?"

"Yes."

"O… okay, then."

"Great!" He gave me a quick peck on my lips this time, thank goodness. Otherwise I might've overheated. "What did you want to say, Rosa?"

"I was going to ask you… if you want to stay the night."

With raised eyebrows, he said, "Really?"

"It's not what you think. No sex. I just… it's been a long time since I slept in a man's arms, and I have an overwhelming desire to sleep in yours. I... I can't believe I just asked you that. I..."

He reached for my hand, squeezed it, and said, "I'd be happy to oblige you."

"Will Julian be okay without you?"

"I'm sure he will. We sleeping in your room?"

"Actually, I thought we could sleep in *this* room."

He smiled as he stood and pulled his dress shirt over his head. Then he bent over and discarded his shoes. In his t-shirt, slacks, and socks, he reached for my hand and led me to the bed.

12
"The Morning After"

I woke up from the sweetest sleep, nestled in the arms of a man I barely knew but shared an undeniable connection with. The scent of his cologne filled my nose as I lifted my head from his chest to glance at his face. His eyes were closed, but he wore a smile as he bent over and kissed my forehead. With his arm wrapped around me, he asked, "Sleep well?"

"Yes, very. You?"

He kissed my forehead again. "Like a baby. But now I'm hungry."

"Hmm, well, let's go see what Dee Dee has cooked up."

"Okay."

I climbed out of bed and reached for his hand. We'd made it to the bedroom door when he swiftly pulled me to him and kissed me for several seconds, his hands slowly sliding up and down my back until he grasped a handful of my blouse and gripped it tightly. When he released me, I was a little light-headed.

"Hmm, still the sweetest sugar I've ever tasted," he murmured.

I blushed as I led him to the kitchen, where we were not greeted by the aroma of bacon or sausage or eggs. Dee Dee was nowhere to be found. Neither was my son. I had no idea where they were.

"Um… Dean, it's been ages since I cooked."

He gave me a lopsided grin and a wink. "I was under the

impression that it was one of those things that once you learn how to do it, you never forget."

"Oh, I haven't forgotten, just can't promise you it'll be good after all this time."

He pulled me into his arms in the middle of the dining room and said, "I am one hundred percent sure it'll be the best I've ever had."

Warmth surged through my body.

"I tell you what, let me take you out for breakfast. I'll run home and take a quick shower and be back before you have a chance to miss me," he suggested.

I gazed into his green eyes and said, "I already miss you."

He pecked me on the lips and left.

After I rushed through a shower, dressed, and put on a little makeup, I sat in the sitting room and smiled. I was happy, so happy that I realized that before Dean, I wasn't all that happy at all. Settled, complacent, maybe even a little content, but not happy. And now that I was happy, I wanted to *stay* happy.

He picked me up in under an hour, dressed in jeans and a flannel shirt, his hair still wet from his shower. In no time, we were heading down the highway to what he described as his favorite breakfast spot, which ended up being a truck stop a few miles up the road from his house.

As we took our seats at a window booth, I said, "How was Julian when you went by your house?"

He sighed and shook his head. "He wasn't home. No telling what he got into last night."

"I'm sorry. I shouldn't have asked you to stay the night."

"Woman, I wouldn't give anything for the pleasure of holding you in my arms last night. I'm coming to realize that Julian is responsible for his own actions. At the end of the day, he's an adult. I can't control him. I can only show him the way. Like you said, he's got to choose to do right. And I can't stop living trying to *make* him choose the right."

I nodded in agreement. "You're right, and I enjoyed sleeping in your arms, too."

He grinned. "Well, we're going to have to make sure we do that more often, Rosa."

"I hope so."

The waitress came and took our orders—Eggs Benedict and wheat toast for me, biscuits, fried eggs, bacon, ham, and grits for him. And he ate every bit of it! Over breakfast, we talked about a few benign things like the weather, gas prices, and how much of an Arkansas Razorback fan he was—all sports.

After the plates were cleared, and over steamy cups of coffee, Dean gave me a serious look and said, "Rosa, I need to tell you something about me, about my past."

Oh, Lord, I thought. *Please don't tell me you're a serial killer or a pedophile or a—*

"My wife and I have been divorced for a long time, close to forty years, and I'm the reason our marriage fell apart."

"W… what did you do?"

He blew out a breath. "I, uh, cheated on her."

"Oh…"

"Look, I'm not trying to make excuses, but that was a long time ago. I was young and stupid, and there is no way I would do anything like that to you. I promise. I just wanted to be up front and totally honest with you because I think we're starting something great."

"Okay."

"You're not upset, leery, nothing?"

"Well, I know what it means to be young and stupid. Freeman's father cheated on his wife, too... with me. It's not something I'm proud of and because of it, I'm in no position to judge you and I hope you won't judge me."

"Really? I mean, no, I won't judge you, but... really?"

"Really. Turned my life upside down. You know, it's amazing that the worst decision I've ever made was also the best decision. When word got out that I was pregnant, I was ostracized. We went to the same church. Our families knew each other. His wife had even been a childhood friend of mine, not a close friend, but a friend nonetheless. And to make matters worse, I was their child's teacher at the time."

"Really?" He shook his head. "I should stop that. I sound like a parrot."

I smiled. "No, I guess to look at me one wouldn't believe I was ever that reckless or stupid. I was as wrong as wrong can get for what I did, and let me tell you, I definitely learned my lesson after I was kicked out of church, fired, and run out of town. My own father disowned me for being a Jezebel—his exact words. And since his word was law, my mama cut ties with me, too. They never really forgave me. They tolerated me for short visits, but that was it."

With a frown on his handsome face, he leaned forward and rested his hands on the table. "What did they do to *him*?"

"Nothing. Absolutely nothing. At one point he was even made a deacon at his church—beloved, respected, and revered by many. But get this: my son isn't his only outside child and I wasn't the first or last of his mistresses. But he was allowed to live the good life while spreading his seed from sea to shining sea, and I was forced to move away from the only home I'd known except for my college years, and raise my son without the benefit of having family there to help me. But God." I shook my head. "He forgave me, helped me every step of the way, and I raised my boy up to be the wonderful, kind, caring, and mischievous man he is today. I wouldn't give anything for him."

"I can tell you raised him well," he said with a warm smile on his face. "So how'd you end up back here?"

"Well, I've always loved the manor from the time I was a child. I hated what it represented, but I loved the beauty of the building and property, the alley of oaks, all of it. I dreamt of owning it and transforming it from a place full of bad memories for my people to a place of comfort and love. I was always talking about it after I moved and I'd drive by and look at it when I returned home from time to time, which was usually only for funerals. And then there were no more funerals to attend, everyone was gone, and so was my connection to Hyacinth Valley and the manor. But I was still talking about it all the time, and well, my son is a man of more action and less talk."

"My kind of guy," Dean said.

"I bet. Well, anyway, he upped and bought it for me, paid for renovations, and the rest is history. I opened up shop and hired a staff and in a way, built a new home and a new family for myself. It was sort of a redemption for me, a way of saying, 'You tried to break me, but look at me now.'"

He reached across the table for my hand and said, "Yes, look at you now."

I smiled. "I'm just glad Freeman's father and his wife have moved. I wouldn't want to have to deal with another smear campaign. It'd ruin my business."

"You think they'd still do something like that to you, even after all these years?"

"Definitely. His wife was never a very kind or forgiving person."

"I see. Well, I'm glad you came back to town—for my sake."

I gave him another smile. "Yeah… me, too." I looked down at our joined hands and added, "Dean, I have to be honest. I've been a little out of sorts lately and I think it's because my little manor family is spreading its wings and flying away from my nest. I've been feeling…"

"Lonely?"

With lifted eyebrows, I said, "Yes. Exactly."

"Me, too, Rosa. Me, too."

"Well, I want to thank you for pursuing me and not giving up even though I gave you reason to."

He rubbed our joined hands with his free one. "Rosa, I might not be the smartest man in the world, but I know a good thing when I see it, and I'm not in the business of letting good things pass me by. If I weren't so ashamed of my grandson for robbing your place, I'd thank him for bringing us together."

"Well, I should confess that I came to your house to meet you because I'd found out you were a descendent of Essie and Richard. Julian being there and me finding out he was your grandson was a big surprise for me."

"Either way, I'm thankful." He stretched across the table and lightly kissed me. "But can I ask you a question?"

"Sure."

"Why didn't you ever marry? I know you had to have had offers."

"The truth?"

He nodded. "Please."

"I've never been in love."

He reclined in his seat and said, "Well, I'm just gonna have to do something about that."

"I look forward to it."

13
"Love Is"

We took a ride to the neighboring town of Paxton and did some window shopping, had a delicious lunch at a small café, and returned to the manor in time for dinner to find Dee Dee and Man in the sitting room, snuggled up on the sofa. They both jumped to their feet like a couple of caught-red-handed teens as soon as we entered the room. "Don't mind us. Carry on," I said as I took Dean's hand and stepped toward the kitchen. From the smell of things, Dee Dee had cooked something good for dinner.

"Wait!" Man said.

"Ohhh, look at you two," Dee Dee crooned.

Dean grinned proudly and placed his arm around my shoulders. I shook my head and said, "Yes, son?"

"Um…" he grabbed Dee Dee's hand and once they'd moved from the sofa to a spot right in front of me, he thrust her left hand in my face. "We got married this morning."

Dean boomed with laughter. "Congratulations, you two! You are definitely a man of action, huh, Freeman?"

Dean and Man embraced. "Call me Man like everyone else, Dean."

"You got it, Man!" Dean said as he released my son and bear-hugged his new wife.

"Wow," was all I could say.

"That's it?" Man said, his eyes on me.

The expression on his face reminded me of when he was a boy and he'd show me his original artwork or his grade on a test. He needed my approval then, and I never let him down—no matter what. That wasn't about to change. I reached up and kissed my son on the cheek, and then I beckoned for both him and Dee Dee to come to me and I embraced them at the same time. "Congratulations, you two. I couldn't be happier for you." And I meant it, and that surprised even me. "Dee Dee, I'm expecting some grandchildren soon," I added.

Once I released them, Dee Dee began to weep. I was almost certain they were tears of relief. "You got it, Ms. Rosa! Like my cousins, Sister Sledge, said, 'We are family!'" she whimpered.

"Are all of them your cousins, baby?" Man asked.

I gave him a look and he shrugged his shoulders as he pulled his bride into his arms.

***

Dean went home that night, but arrived bright and early the next morning to have breakfast with me, and after breakfast, we took a walk along the trail that snaked through the woods behind the manor. We walked hand-in-hand, in comfortable silence among the majestic trees. I glanced at him a few times, thought to myself how ironic it was that I was so very attracted to someone I only a short time earlier saw as my enemy. Life was unpredictable, to say the least.

When we came upon the old slave quarters that once served at

August's home, Dean stopped and stared at the log structure.

"It used to be a slave cabin. It's the only one left on the property," I said. "I had it fixed up as a remembrance of my people."

"Did some of your people… were they enslaved here, Rosa?"

I shook my head. "Not that I know of, but I consider all black people my people."

Dean released my hand and moved closer. After appraising the building for a few minutes, he took a seat on the bottom of the porch. I sat down next to him. "I can't say what I would've done if I was alive back then," he said. "I hope I would've been man enough to do what Richard did and leave this mess behind. I hope I would've had the same heart and mind I do today and have always had. It was wrong, Rosa. Dead wrong. Slavery was as far away from right as one can get and I am ashamed that anyone who ever shared my blood thought it was right. And don't think I don't know what all happened. My daughter is a historian, has tons of slave narratives and other documents, and I've read many of them. I've also watched *Twelve Years a Slave*."

"If you watched that movie, you are far braver than me. I was too afraid of my reaction if I'd watched it. Didn't want to end up in jail for killing random white people."

"I wanted to kill a few myself. I'm embarrassed to carry this last name."

"Don't be. Don't forget that Richard carried that name, too, and he was a good man. And as I'm learning, you are not responsible for what your ancestors did—right or wrong. And at least you've educated yourself and have an ounce of empathy. I'm impressed."

"Thank you."

"But I have to say this, Dean. As long as I live, I will fight for what is right for my people. *Always.*"

"I wouldn't expect any less of you, Rosa. It's what's right, and I wanna be right by your side, supporting and helping you."

I felt a swelling inside of me that I can't quite describe.

We were quiet for a few moments before he grabbed my hand and squeezed it. "I'm glad you decided to give us a chance."

"Hmm, me, too."

More silence.

"Dean?"

"Yes?"

"Would you mind kissing me?"

As he leaned in closer with his eyes on my lips, he said, "It'd be my pleasure."

***

After a month of being courted by Dean Jarsdel, I finally had firsthand knowledge of what it felt like to nose-dive into love. This man held my hand, kissed my lips, and little by little, chipped away at a wall I never even realized had been surrounding my heart. I'd never loved Man's father, but the ordeal with him had hardened me in ways I never knew or comprehended. I'd dated men, I'd bedded men, but now I fully realized that the true reason I'd never fallen in love is that I'd never allowed myself to. Well, Dean Jarsdel owned the magic keys—patience and persistence—and with them, he'd opened a part of my heart that had been bound with old, rusty chains for a long, long time. It had taken a little elbow grease, but he'd worked his way into my heart and made a home there… and he was more than welcome.

One night we sat on his front porch while Julian played video games in his room, and we watched the cars pass by on the highway. We sat in separate lawn chairs, holding hands and sipping lemonade. Spring had fully sprung and there was a peace surrounding us that I loved. I loved being with him more than anything in the world at that point, and the thought of being without him never entered my mind.

"You know what I wanna do?" he asked.

"Hmm, kiss me?"

He grinned and then leaned toward me and kissed me sweetly. "I always wanna do that, pretty lady. I was thinking I wanna take you to this cabin I have up toward Branson."

"I thought you knew me better than that. I'm not the rugged type, sugar."

"I love it when you call me that."

I gave him a sly look. "You do… *sugar*?"

"I do. Makes me wanna do things to you."

"Like what?"

He scooted his chair closer to mine, leaned in, and whispered a whole list of naughty things in my ear, so naughty that my ancient body began to overheat.

"Dean Jarsdel! You are a bad boy!"

He caught my chin and kissed me deeply. "Hmm, I'm *your* bad boy."

I fanned myself with my hand. "You keep talking like that and I'll never call you Dean again. You'll be sugar twenty-four-seven."

"It's more than talk, honey, you just wait and see. And the cabin is not what you think. It's a house with electricity and running water, all the comforts of home. It's just situated far away from the hustle and bustle of the world."

I shrugged, my eyes on the road in front of the house. "I don't know."

"I'll do all of the cooking. Hell, I'll pay someone to cook."

"You act like I can't cook. I can cook, sugar."

"Coulda fooled me."

I turned to face him. "I *don't* cook, not *can't* cook. There's a difference."

With a twinkle in his eyes, he said, "If you say so, pretty lady."

"Keep on, and you're gonna get yourself in trouble."

He lowered his voice. "You gonna spank me or something?"

I raised an eyebrow. "You want me to?"

He glanced at the front door. "If Julian wasn't here…"

"If Julian wasn't here, *nothing*. I'm a lady."

"And I'm a gentleman who loves this lady."

I reached for his hand and squeezed it. "I love you, too, sugar."

14
"We Are One"

"*What* did you say this was we're going to that required me to wear this thing?" Dean said as he navigated the heavy Little Rock traffic.

I reached over and tugged on the collar of his tuxedo jacket. "A benefit. One of my best patrons and supporters is on the committee and she sent me tickets, practically begged me to come. And Mr. Jarsdel, you look handsome in that thing, sugar. *Very* handsome."

He shot me a grin. "Woman, when you stepped into the sitting room wearing that dress, I think my heart stopped, I almost needed to be resuscitated. You. Look. Beautiful."

I glanced down at my red dress. "You keep saying that and I might start believing you really mean it."

"You better believe I mean it. And don't you sit over there and pretend a man never told you that before."

"I didn't say that."

"I know I'm not the first to say it or think it, but I plan to be the last man in this position to say it."

I faced him and said, "What position?"

"The position of being the only man in your life."

"Hmm."

He slowed the car a bit and glanced at me. "What did that mean? I *am* the only man in your life, right?"

I reached over and rubbed my hand over the neatly trimmed hair of his beard. "Only you… and Freeman."

I could see him relax. He chuckled. "I don't mind sharing you with him, but *only* him."

"You two are all I need, sugar."

We arrived right on time, were personally greeted by Gail Hart, my patron, and led to a table near the head table, situated on the edge of the parquet dancefloor. We took our seats, held hands, sipped on the wine that was sitting in the center of our table, and chatted quietly as our table and the room began to fill.

"This is nice," Dean said, taking in the elegant décor. "And this event benefits a homeless shelter?"

"Yes, Gail lost a sister who was homeless. She was mentally ill and disappeared for some years. She died from exposure one winter."

"Hmm, well, I'll be sure to make a donation before we leave since the tickets were free."

"Me, too."

He squeezed my hand. "I'll make one for both of us. I'll just double what I was going to give."

"That would be *you* giving, not me."

"As far as I'm concerned, we're one, pretty lady. What I give, you give."

I leaned in close and kissed him. "That might be why I love you."

"Or it might be because I loved you first."

"Always trying to one up me."

He smiled and gently tapped my nose. "You'll never love me more than I love you, Rosa, so stop trying."

"Well, I see they seated us with a couple of lovebirds, honey," a voice said—a *familiar* voice. I looked up and nearly fell out of my seat. Standing behind the only two vacant chairs left at our table was Jeanine Noble. Next to her stood her husband, my son's father, the one and only Lawrence Noble. They apparently were as shocked as I was because they both just stood there, mouths agape, both pairs of eyes on me. "Rosa Lee Stark?" Jeanine said after several seconds of muteness.

"Hi, Jeanine," I said. I didn't bother speaking to Lawrence and didn't wait for Jeanine to reply. Instead, I turned back to Dean and blew out a breath. He frowned slightly, shifting his eyes from me to Lawrence, and back. He lifted his eyebrows and mouthed, "Oh." I was sure he'd noticed that Lawrence and Man were virtually twins except for the fact that Lawrence was older, a hair taller, heavier, and bald.

Lawrence left and was back in a matter of minutes, leaning close to his wife and whispering something in her ear. I was sure he'd requested a change of seats and had been denied since the place was packed and the program was about to start.

Dean wrapped his arm around my shoulder and pulled me so close, I had to scoot my chair over to keep from falling to the floor. "Hey, you okay?" he whispered.

"I'm with you, sugar. Of course I'm okay."

He kissed me on the lips for what felt like five or six minutes, and then he gave me a smile. I could feel the Nobles' eyes searing my back, but I didn't turn around.

A delicious dinner was served, inspiring speeches were recited, large checks were presented, and then the musical guest—the real reason most folks had paid five hundred dollars a plate to be there—was introduced.

Dean didn't know this, but the musical guest was the only reason I decided to accept Gail's invitation. This definitely wasn't the first year she'd gifted me with tickets, but in the past, I'd declined and shown my support by mailing a check. After all, I didn't have an escort before, and who would want to sit alone all night amongst a room packed largely with couples?

This year was different. This year, I had Dean, and the musical guest was none other than Maze featuring Frankie Beverly. Frankie and Maze were the reason I didn't leave when I found out I was sharing a table with the Nobles. No way was I missing out on seeing my favorite group perform live for the first time in my life. No way!

When the MC presented them, I was the first to leap to my feet and applaud. Dean stood beside me with a huge grin on his face. He liked Maze, too. Well, he liked a wide variety of music from bluegrass to rock and roll.

We danced in our seats through two songs, then hit the dancefloor when they began to play "Joy and Pain." I finally got to see Dean in action. He wasn't a half-bad dancer and managed to stay pretty much on beat, but all the cheering my family did in the backyard was definitely exaggerated.

We danced through a couple more up-tempo songs before they slowed it down with "Happy Feelin's," and Dean pulled me into his arms. I rested my head on his chest, breathed in the scent of his cologne, felt the warmth of his body, and closed my eyes. I'd found that in his arms was my favorite place to be. I couldn't wait until the day when I never had to leave them, when we could share a home and combine our lives forever. At that moment, I realized I wanted that more than anything in the world—to be Mrs. Richard Dean Jarsdel.

As the song ended, Dean whispered in my ear, "I'm going to find the restroom."

I nodded and glanced over at our table, which was empty. "Go ahead, I'll be at our table."

He cradled my face in his hands and kissed me. "You sure you'll be okay?"

"I'll be fine. Hurry back."

"Will do."

I reclaimed my seat and smiled at the others who were gliding around the dancefloor to "Back in Stride." I glanced toward the direction of the restrooms a couple of times, hoping Dean would make it back before Frankie sang "Can't Get Over You," which was one of my favorites. When I turned my head to see that Lawrence Noble and his loud cologne had returned to the table, I wished I'd gone to the ladies' room just to kill time instead of coming back to the table. I was looking around the room, purposely ignoring him, when I heard him say, "It's good to see you, Rosa."

I turned and looked at him, then shifted my attention to Frankie onstage. Wasn't any point in me lying in reciprocation. I honestly could've gone an eternity without seeing his trifling behind.

"Don't be like that. I just wanted to tell you how good you look. Still got those big pretty legs, I see. Man, you have always been and still are one fine woman! Reminds me of the old days just seeing you. You still a tigress in bed?"

I rolled my eyes. "My goodness! Aren't you too old to still be doing this? I mean, are you even still... *capable*? What? Do you have a pump or a prescription for extra strength Viagra or something?"

"Aw, now, baby girl. Don't be mean. I just want some of that goodness of yours."

"Where is your wife?"

"In the restroom."

I was glad I didn't go in there after all. "Why don't you go see about her, help her wipe her butt or something?"

"How is... everything?" he asked, ignoring my question.

I twisted around in my seat and fixed my eyes on him. "*Everything* is fine. As a matter of fact, *everything* is all grown up, married, and one hell of a businessman—one hell of a man, *period*. Thanks for the child support, by the way."

He dropped his eyes and cleared his throat. "Um... yeah. So what's with you and the white guy? Last I knew of you, you hated white folks, were pretty emphatic about it. Did he come with that plantation I heard you bought or something? Y'all got some slaves?" He chuckled.

"You know, I'd expect an ancient plantation stud to say something like that."

"A what?"

"Look it up. You might learn something about yourself."

"Look, all I'm saying is I'm a little shocked to see you with a white man. I mean, you? I never would've thought..."

I smiled. "Hmm… well, that must make him one hell of a man then, huh?"

He sighed. "Rosa—"

A hand appeared between us, cutting off Lawrence's words. "I'm Dean Jarsdel. Rosa's told me a lot about you."

Lawrence stood and took Dean's hand. "Jarsdel? Didn't some Jarsdels own that plantation at one point?"

Dean nodded and lowered his voice. "Sure did, but I've never been into real estate. I'm a retired Navy Seal. Clandestine operations. Killed many men with my bare hands for my country. Wouldn't hesitate to do the same thing for my Rosa, so you just watch yourself. You understand?" There was so much venom in his voice, he scared *me* a little.

Lawrence snatched his hand away and turned to leave, bumping right into his wife. "Honey, what's wrong?" she asked her obviously nervous husband, and then she cut her eyes at me. "What did she say?"

"What?" I said. I was surprised, but I shouldn't have been. She hadn't changed. Nothing would ever be Lawrence's fault in her eyes.

"I said, what did you say? Isn't it enough that you tried to ruin my marriage once? You need to take yourself and your white man and leave us alone!" she hissed.

"Now, wait a minute," Dean began.

I stood from my seat and placed a hand on his chest. I shook my head and whispered, "It's okay, sugar." Then I turned my attention to Jeanine Noble. "You know what, I'm not going to cause a scene at my friend's event," I said through clenched teeth, felt Dean rest his hand on my arm. "But I will say something I've been meaning to say for over forty years: I am sorry, Jeanine, for sleeping with your husband. I really am. I was dead wrong, but so was he. I might've been a ho', but at least I changed my ways. Now, that husband of yours is a different story. And let me give you a little advice: you better leash his old ass before he brings home more than fleas." I grabbed my clutch from the table and my man's hand, kissed him and said, "I'm ready to leave if you are."

He grinned. "Lead the way, pretty lady."

***

"Oh, my feet! Been a long time since I danced in heels like these," I said as I stepped out of my shoes and collapsed onto the foot of the bed in our suite. I looked up to see an uncharacteristically quiet Dean standing by the door staring at the bed. "What's wrong?" I asked.

He leaned against the door. "I respect you, Rosa, more than I have any other woman, but I don't know how many more times I can sleep in the same bed with you and not—*you know*."

"I don't know how many more times I can do it, either, with that body and face of yours, and at our ages, it's really kind of foolish to keep waiting like this."

"So you mean—you wanna get married, Rosa? I don't have a ring—"

My heart felt like it jumped out of my chest and then fell back into place. "I want to marry you more than anything."

"Really? You wanna do it tomorrow?"

"I wish we could do it tonight, but my feet..."

He smiled, dropped his keys on the bedside table, and then sat on the bed. He took my left foot in his hand and softly kissed each toe. As he began massaging my foot, he said, "You even have beautiful feet."

I lay back and sighed. "Thank you and ohhhh, that feels so good, sugar."

"My pleasure. And after I get these feet to feeling better, we're gonna get some sleep and head back home early in the morning. We can get the license in Paxton and go to a justice of the peace there. Freeman, Dee Dee, and Julian can stand with us."

"I can't wait. I love you so much, Dean."

"I believe I love you more, Rosa, and by the way, tonight was the first time I've heard you swear."

I closed my eyes and shook my head. "I know. I don't usually use that kind of language. I really consider myself to be a lady. I'm sorry."

"No, don't apologize. It turned me on."

I sat up and swatted at him and he chuckled.

15
"Happy Feelin's"

I was nervous on the ride back to Hyacinth Valley. Sure, I was no spring chicken, but I'd never been married before, and the idea of becoming a new bride at sixty-two was daunting and exciting at the same time. I loved Dean, but what kind of husband would he be? What kind of wife would I be, for that matter? We'd spent the night discussing our future lives together. He'd move into the manor with me, let Julian stay in his house until he decided what he wanted to do with his life. Dean was retired and was happy to help me run the manor and take up some of the duties that Man was now helping me with. He was excited and a large part of me was, too. One thing I was sure of with every fiber of my being was that this was the right thing to do. Nervous or not, I loved this man and didn't want to spend a day without him for the rest of my life.

"Penny for your thoughts, pretty lady?" Dean said.

I smiled. "Just thinking about what it's going to be like to be your wife."

"I'm gonna make sure it's the best thing that ever happened to you, I can assure you of that. I love you, and I'm gonna make it my job to put a smile on your face every day."

"You already do that, sugar. Every day."

"You do the same for me, honey. Every hour of every day."

"There you go one-upping me again."

He shrugged. "It's the truth."

"Hey, I meant to ask you this earlier: did you really kill men with your bare hands?"

He chuckled as he glanced at me and then returned his attention to the road. "Why? Are you scared of me now?"

"No, if anything, you make me feel safer than I ever have in my life."

"I'm glad to hear that. Let's just say I did some things during my time in the military that could make you question my Christianity, all in the name of Lady Liberty... but usually with a gun."

I frowned, adjusted in my seat, wasn't sure how to respond.

"All of that's in the past, now. Been retired for close to ten years. If I had to do it all over again, I'd be an accountant, something boring and safe."

"No, sir, I could never see you as boring—ever. Dean, did you mean what you said to Lawrence or was that just an idle threat?"

He raised an eyebrow as he shook his head. "I don't make idle threats, Rosa. Rest assured, if need be, I would gladly make him disappear. I love you, and what I love, I protect."

I nodded as I gazed out the window, my heart swelling with love for this man.

***

"Okay, pretty lady. Be ready in an hour."

I kissed him and said, "I will. Can't wait to become your wife."

"Love you, see you soon."

"Love you, too."

I stood on the porch and watched him drive away in his Cadillac, which he reserved for special occasions like the benefit and later, for our nuptials. I sauntered into the house and closed the door behind me, sighing as I made my way to my room. I knew just what I was going to wear and had even mentally picked out the jewelry that would best complement the dress. I was feeling giddy by the time I opened my bedroom door and stepped inside, but when I saw a figure sitting on the side of my bed, I almost jumped out of my skin.

"Man! What in the world are you doing in here?"

"I saw y'all pull up. Wanted to know how Frankie and Maze were."

"Shouldn't you be somewhere cuddled up with your new wife?" I asked.

He got to his feet and walked over to where I stood by the door, gave me a curious look. "What's going on?"

I frowned. "What do you mean?" I reached up and touched my face. "Is there something wrong with my face?"

"No... you look... *happy*."

I rolled my eyes. "So what are you saying, that I usually look *unhappy*?"

He shook his head. "No... not unhappy, just serious. You've always looked so serious, for as long as I can remember."

I shrugged. "Maybe it's because I'm getting married today."

With wide eyes, he said, "What?!" He grabbed me and pulled me into a hug, lifting me from the floor. "Mama, I'm so happy for you and Dean!" He set me down. "Wait, you *are* marrying Dean, right?"

"Of course. Who else? I take it you approve of him?"

"He's the *only* man I'd approve of you marrying. He loves you, Mama. He really does."

I floated over to my bed and took a seat. "I know, and I love him."

"This is great, Mama. Let me go tell Dee Dee. She's gonna have a fit."

"Well, you two get dressed. You're going to the justice of the peace with us. Dean's coming to pick me up in an hour."

"Okay, we'll trail you guys." He rushed from my room, yelling, "Dee Dee!"

I lay back on my bed for a moment with a smile on my face before taking a shower and preparing myself to become Mrs. Dean Jarsdel.

16
"Joy and Pain"

He stood me up.

An hour passed and no Dean. There I sat in the sitting room, dressed in my favorite white Grecian dress, my afro on point, my jewelry matched to perfection, face beat like never before, and… no Dean. The silence in the room as Dee Dee and Man waited with me was deafening. I called his cell—no answer. I called his home phone—no answer. And as I sat there watching the pendulum swing back and forth on the old grandfather clock across the room, I was filled with dread and fear and disappointment. One minute, I thought he'd changed his mind. The next minute, I knew better, but thought something had happened to him. Then I wondered if I had dreamt the whole conversation, the plans, the declarations of love. Along with my gifts, had I lost my mind?

I closed my eyes and prayed for him to show up and that once he arrived, he'd have some funny story to tell about a flat tire or something as benign as that. But the more I prayed, the more time slipped by without a word from him, and the more a sense of panic rose from my gut and screamed in my head.

"Maybe he's having car trouble," Dee Dee offered.

I just nodded. I was in no condition to respond verbally. I was on the verge of tears. I felt a very ugly cry coming on, because if I didn't know anything else, I knew that man loved me and wanted to marry me. I felt that in my soul.

Man stood, grabbed his keys.

"Where are you going?" Dee Dee asked, parroting my thoughts.

"To Dean's. He might be on the side of the road needing help. Maybe his cell is dead or something."

Dee Dee nodded as I watched him leave and tried to empty my mind of the thought that his cell might not have been the only thing that was dead.

"Ms. Rosa, can I get you anything?" she asked.

I shook my head and was about to tell her that I was going to go lie down in my room when my own cell phone rang. I jumped a little at the chiming ring tone and stared at the hand that held the phone. Dean's cell number popped onto the screen and I nearly dropped my phone in the process of answering it. I held it to my ear with a shaky hand, answered with, "Dean? Where are you, sugar? I've been wait—"

"Ms. Rosa? It's Julian. Can you meet us at the hospital?"

I jumped to my feet and almost fell in my heels. Dee Dee jumped up, too. "Hospital?! What-who-what's going on? Where's your grandfather?" I nearly screamed into the phone.

Julian almost instantly began to sob into the phone. "He's hurt. He's hurt really bad and it's my fault. I'm so sorry. I'm so sorry…"

"Julian! What is going on? What do you mean he's hurt?"

"He got beat up and he's in bad shape. I'm getting in the ambulance with him now. Please meet us at the hospital. Wait—he's trying to say something… Sir? Yes, sir, this is her… Okay. He wants to say something to you."

Tears had already worked their way down my cheeks and I was shaking like a leaf. "Okay, put him on. Dean?"

"Rosa," he slurred. "Rosa, I'm sorry. I love you. I'm sorry…"

Then I heard yelling and Julian's voice filled my ears as he screamed, "He stopped breathing!"

17
"I Love You Too Much"

My eyes were nearly swollen shut from the constant flow of tears I shed between my home and the hospital in Paxton. Dee Dee had called and told Man to meet us there and then she somehow managed to lead me out to her car and drive me there. The ride was a hazy blur with my mind racing with thoughts of my man, the man I loved, lying cold on a stretcher. The thought of no longer seeing his smile or hearing his voice or feeling his touch made my stomach lurch and my heart ache. Surely life wouldn't be this cruel to me— let me find him and lose him before he was ever really mine. Surely after all these years of running away from love, it wouldn't be snatched away from me the moment I decided to accept it.

Surely not.

Julian met us in front of the hospital, relief in his reddened eyes as he spied me. He collapsed into my arms, looking for support that I was honestly in no shape to give him. I somehow managed to ask, "Is he breathing now?"

He nodded. "They did CPR in the ambulance."

I heaved a sigh of relief and felt the tears refill my eyes. "Where is he?"

"In surgery. I'll take you to the waiting room."

We'd been sitting in the waiting room for several minutes before Man joined us and asked Julian what I hadn't the presence of mind to ask. "Julian, what happened?"

All eyes were on Julian now as he lifted his weary head and fixed guilty eyes on me. "Um…. there's this guy I hang out with sometimes. Grandpa doesn't know him, never met him, but you met him, Ms. Rosa."

I frowned. "Who is he?"

"He's the person who hit you during the robbery. There were two of us. It was actually his idea to rob the place. I just went along because he said it was easy money and he would make sure no one was there. When you showed up, he panicked and hit you from behind. I guess you couldn't see him. I didn't tell anyone it was him because he's crazy and I didn't want him to come after me for snitching. Anyway, I stopped hanging with him after that, decided I wasn't about that life after all."

He took a deep breath and blew it out. "He showed up last night with some beer and weed and we kicked it for a while. I shouldn't have let him in. I don't even know why I did. I guess I just wanted to have a little fun since Grandpa was gone. Well, he was still there when Grandpa got back this morning and Grandpa blew up, yelled at him to get out, got on to me, too. My friend got smart with Grandpa and tried to hit him and well, you know my grandpa ain't no punk. He beat dude up and literally threw him out of the house. Then he told me he'd deal with me after… after your wedding. The dude—Jay Dub is his name—Jay Dub was waiting on us when we walked out the house. He ambushed us, beat Grandpa with a bat. When I tried to stop him, he hit me in the back with the bat and knocked me down. He kept hitting Grandpa, calling him names. He… he hit him in the head and in the legs, stomped him." Julian broke down. Man went over to him to comfort him, and I just sat there with wet eyes before standing on unsteady legs.

"Mama, where you going?" Man asked.

"To talk to the only somebody who can fix this."

***

In the hospital's small chapel, I prayed and travailed and begged God for Dean's life. I fell on my knees at the altar and pressed my face into the carpeted floor and moaned and groaned and pleaded for mercy.

"God, my gift is gone, and my family is blowing away like chaff in the wind. Please, Father, please don't let me lose Dean, too. God, please. If I have ever done anything pleasing in Your eyes, save him. Please, save him."

And as clear as day, I heard a voice say, "Your gift was for an appointed time. You fulfilled your purpose with it and blessed others. Now it's time for you to be blessed. Love is eternal. Remember that."

I wiped tears and opened my eyes. "Lord, if it is Your will, can we start our eternity together on Earth? Please, Sir. *Please.* Let my blessing be in his healing."

The next voice I heard came from behind me and belonged to Dee Dee. "Ms. Rosa, he's out of surgery now and in ICU. They say you can go see him."

***

I was used to seeing his powerful form in motion, a smile on his face, a quip or a kiss for me on his lips. I was used to feeling one of his powerful hands encasing mine or resting on my back or cupping my face. I was used to a man of sixty-five who still rose with the sun and ran a mile a day, a man in top physical condition with bulging biceps. I was used to a handsome face and green eyes that saw through me. What I was not used to was seeing him lying helpless in a hospital bed with a machine breathing for him, unconscious to the world. His skin was warm, but it was uncharacteristic of him not to squeeze my hand when I held his. I leaned in and kissed his cheek and thought about the many times I'd felt his lips on mine. I wished I could crawl into the bed and rest in his arms.

"Dean," I said softly. "It's Rosa. I'm here, sugar."

He didn't move or blink an eye.

One tear rolled down my cheek. "I love you. No matter what, I love you."

I heard footsteps behind me and looked up to see a pale-skinned, dark-haired doctor standing in the doorway. "Oh, I'm sorry. They told me his fiancée was here and wanted to see me."

I nodded as I wiped my cheek. "I'm his fiancée."

He gave me a surprised look. "Oh… well, I'm Dr. Trenton."

I stood and moved closer to him. "Rosa Stark."

"Okay, Ms. Stark, his left leg is broken as are a couple of his ribs. He also suffered some serious internal injuries and we had to go in and relieve some pressure on his brain. At this point, all we can do is monitor him and hope for the best."

I glanced back at Dean and said, "Thank you for your honesty, doctor."

Then I went back to my seat by his bed and rested my head on the mattress beside him. I could feel the doctor watching us for a while before he left. What he'd said had no bearing on me. I had prayed. I would keep praying. I had to believe that this was not our fate. I had to believe that God would heal him.

I closed my eyes and whispered, "Please God," for the hundredth time, and then I spoke softly to Dean. "You know I told you I'd never been in love before. You're my first love, Dean, my first and only, my soul mate. I never told you this, but God directed me to find you. Well, He directed me to find a relative of Essie and Richard, and my search led me to you. I had no idea why He led me to find you at first, but now I know. In His unending goodness, He looked down and saw how lonely I was and that you were what I needed, and He sent me to you. And isn't it just like God to send me the love of my life in a form I was not expecting, to send me someone to teach me about love and life and humanity just when I thought I knew it all?

"So you see, you have to wake up. You have to live, because we've got a lot of living to do together. I love you so much, sugar. Please wake up."

18
"Can't Stop The Love"

I only left that man's side when they made me. Even when his gorgeous daughter and handsome son came, I stayed. I spent the night in the hospital, refused to go home even to change, so Dee Dee brought some of my clothes from home and I would take wash ups in the public restrooms. Man and Dee Dee would bring me food, and I'd eat with them and Dean's kids in the waiting room. After being encouraged to do so by Man, Julian called the police and gave them his friend's name. He was arrested and had confessed, and thank goodness, he'd be spending a good amount of time in jail.

The doctor came in every day for two weeks and reported the same thing—no change. And I kept praying and reading The Word to Dean. When I would drift off to sleep, I'd pray in my dreams. And finally, on a sunny Saturday, Dean Jarsdel opened his eyes and smiled at me. And when they removed the breathing tube two days later, his first words to me were, "You ready to get married?"

I wanted to marry him right there in his hospital room with him in that bed. He refused, said we were going to do it right since this was my first and last wedding, said I deserved only the best. Considering what he'd just been through, what I'd just gone through with him, I didn't want to wait, but he insisted.

He was the hardest-working man in physical therapy, pushed himself beyond any reasonable limits so that he could stand at the altar with me. I told him it didn't matter if he was on crutches or sitting in a wheelchair or whatever, but it mattered to Dean. So three months after he was injured, I found myself being escorted toward him by my son with everyone I loved standing as witnesses. As I passed the smiling faces of Rochelle and Teo, who serenaded me down the aisle, and of August who held his baby son as his wife beamed at me, and a visibly happy Dorcas with Farris, I knew Dean was right. This was what I really and truly deserved—to marry the love of my life in the backyard of my beloved manor with my family surrounding me, family that included a pregnant Dee Dee. Yes, I was finally becoming a grandmother!

Man presented me to Dean, whose eyes shone with tears as he took my hand and kissed my cheek. He smiled at me, looking handsome in his suit. I glanced over at Julian and his mother and took a deep breath. Dean's son Brandon even made it. This was the first day in my forever with Dean and as we exchanged vows, I silently thanked God for shining His face on me and loving me so much that He'd take the time to make this man for me and at the right time, allow our paths to collide.

Before the preacher could finish proclaiming, "I now pronounce you man and wife," Dean had already pulled me into his arms, whispered, "You're mine now," and laid a monumental kiss on me.

We partied into the night, and when we finally retired to my room and commenced with the honeymoon, I felt like a kid on Christmas morning, like I was finally getting to unwrap a gift I'd been staring at under the Christmas tree since December first, a gift I'd begged for and was sure I was going to enjoy. The anticipation of consummating my relationship with Dean was nearly unbearable. I was nervous and excited all at the same time. And of all times, he wanted to take things slowly and prolong my torture. He gingerly undressed me, smiled as he revealed my skin inch by inch. "Beautiful," he whispered. "Absolutely beautiful."

"My turn," I softly said as he kissed my neck. I undressed him, revealing a physique that was still impressive even after him having been bedbound for so long. I kissed his chest, felt him tremble beneath my touch, and after he was fully undressed, we showed each other what we both had learned about lovemaking over the years and enjoyed the pleasure of mature, experienced love. His loving was good, the best I'd ever had—hands down.

As I lay in his arms early the next morning, I rubbed my hand on his chest and sighed. Being there with him was Heaven to me.

"You awake?" he asked.

"Mm-hmm. You should be sleep, though. You've got to drive us up to the cabin in a few hours."

"I know, but I want some more of what I had earlier…"

"It's yours. All you have to do is come and get it, sugar."

"You remember what I told you about calling me that? What it makes me wanna do?"

"Mm-hmm, and I'm hoping you're a man of your word."

He rolled me over onto my back, smiled down at me, and said, "Oh, I am."

Epilogue

My husband had me pinned to the wall behind the front desk, his mouth covering mine when we both heard the front door open and shut. He reluctantly released me and I attempted to compose myself as the young, blond-headed woman approached us. She settled her weary blue eyes on us and said, "I saw the sign on the street, been driving all day, and was wondering if you all had any vacancies. I'm on my way to Louisiana for a friend's wedding."

I gave her a warm smile. "What's your name, dear?"

"Amanda... Amanda Burkes."

"Well, Amanda, you look like you could use some rest, so of course we have a room for you." I turned my attention to Dean. "Honey, you wanna get her checked in?"

Dean smiled. "It'd be my pleasure."

As Dean swiped her credit card, the young lady said, "You two look nice together. Must feel good to be that much in love."

I nodded and pecked Dean on the cheek. "It feels wonderful."

She sighed. "I hope I'll know what that feels like one day. I'm almost forty and this'll be my fifth time being a bridesmaid for one of my friends. I've just about given up hope."

As I led her to Room Ten, I said, "You never know. Love just might be right around the corner for you."

For information about racial unity and reconciliation, visit:

http://beabridgebuilder.com/

For more information about Adrienne Thompson, visit:

http://adriennethompsonwrites.webs.com

Sign up for Adrienne's newsletter here: http://eepurl.com/jnDmH

Follow Adrienne on Twitter!

https://twitter.com/A_H_Thompson

Like Adrienne on Facebook!

https://www.facebook.com/AdrienneThompsonWrites

Join Adrienne's Facebook group!!

https://www.facebook.com/groups/674088779363625/

Follow Adrienne on Pinterest!

http://www.pinterest.com/ahthompsn/

Connect with Adrienne on Goodreads!

https://www.goodreads.com/author/show/5051327.Adrienne_Th

ompson

After the Pain

No Pain, No Gain

Joy and Pain

Stand-alone novels:

Home

See Me

When You've Been Blessed (Feels Like Heaven)

Summertime (A Novella)

Fiction Anthology:

The Ex Chronicles – as a contributor

Nonfiction Titles:

Just Between Us (Inspiring Stories by Women) –as a contributor

Seven Days of Change (A Flash Devotional)

Poetry:

Poetry from the Soul… for the Soul, Volume II

All books are available at amazon.com, barnesandnoble.com, and kobobooks.com

I LAY ASLEEP, SECURE IN MY HUSBAND'S ARMS, WHEN HIS cell phone rang. By then, I was used to late night calls from church members reporting that a loved one was sick or had entered the hospital or had passed away. I even kept an outfit hanging in the closet in case Apollo and I had to make an unexpected trip in the middle of the night. But the calls usually came to the house phone. Only church officials or family members had his cell number. I lifted my head up from his chest and shook his shoulder.

"Apollo, your phone's ringing," I said.

"Hmm?" he responded groggily.

"Honey, your phone's ringing. You want me to get it?"

He shook his head and rubbed his eyes. "No, I'll get it. No sense in both of us having to break our rest." *My rest is already broken*, I thought.

Apollo kissed my forehead then sat up on the side of the bed to pull on his boxers and a t-shirt as he answered the phone.

"Hello?" he said. He listened to the caller for a moment and then said, "Alright, hold on a minute."

He stood and left the room. I lay back down and closed my eyes but found it impossible to fall back to sleep. My mind was reeling, wondering who was on the phone and what had happened. Finally, I sat up on the side of the bed and wrapped my robe around the fleshy curves of my body. I ran my hand through the soft twists on my head and slid my feet into my slippers.

I headed out of the room, having decided to get a glass of water from the kitchen. I walked down the hall towards the winding staircase and as I passed our son AJ's room, noticed that his light was on. *I guess he finally made it home,* I thought as I peeped through the slightly open door. It was Apollo, not AJ, who was in the room. Apollo was sitting on the side of AJ's bed with his back to the door having a rather hushed conversation on the phone. I stood there for a moment and then told myself not to eavesdrop. *He'll tell me about it when he hangs up. He always does.*

I continued to the kitchen, fixed a glass of water, and headed back up the stairs. This time when I passed by AJ's room, I could hear Apollo raising his voice. I stopped by the door and listened.

"Don't you ever call me at this time of night again, you understand? And you sure as hell better not come to my house. We'll deal with this later," he said in a harsh whisper.

I raised my eyebrows and wondered who he was talking to and what he was talking about. I stood there for a few more seconds, but he lowered his voice and I couldn't make out what he was saying. Not wanting to get caught eavesdropping, I headed to the bedroom and settled back into the bed. A few minutes later, Apollo returned to our bedroom, climbed into the bed, and spooned himself behind me.

"Who was that?" I asked.

"Nobody, one of the deacons about some program. Go back to sleep, baby."

I frowned. "A deacon at this time of night? Which deacon?"

"Yeah, I'm gonna have a talk with him in the morning." He only half answered my question.

He snuggled closer to me and kissed my shoulder. I opened my mouth to reply but then decided against it. I was pretty positive that Apollo was lying, but I didn't want to argue. We never argued, and I liked it that way. I closed my eyes and tried to sleep, but couldn't. That phone call and what I'd heard Apollo saying to the caller was all I could think of. I lay there wide awake for what felt like hours listening to Apollo's breathing and finally, having waited as long as I could, slipped out of the bed and quietly walked around to pick Apollo's phone up from the night table.

I tipped out into the hallway. I shook my head and thought, *Lord, I can't believe I'm checking his phone. We've been married for twenty years, and I'm checking his phone like some kind of jealous crazy person.*

"I'm not doing this," I whispered to myself. I turned back towards our bedroom door but couldn't make myself move. *Okay, I'll just check it and see that it was one of the deacons like he said, and then I can get some sleep.* I took a deep breath and then clicked the button on Apollo's phone until his call log popped up.